HEARTS
UNLEASHED

ALSO BY JULIA DUMONT:

Sleeping With Dogs and Other Lovers,
A Second Acts Novel - Book 1

Starstruck Romance and Other Hollywood Tails,
A Second Acts Novel - Book 2

"The misunderstandings and mischief will keep readers turning pages... erotic adventure for readers more interested in an entertaining read than deep thought."
— *Kirkus Reviews* of Book 1

"Dumont's second foray into the turbulent, sexy, often-hilarious world of celebrity dating provides a delightful diversion. A sexy romp through glamorous modern Hollywood as seen through the eyes of a self-possessed matchmaker who cannot find her own match."
— *Kirkus Reviews* of Book 2

"Think Stephanie Plum meets *Sex and the City* wearing *Fifty Shades of Grey* – L.A. style. In Julia Dumont's funny and erotic romantic novel, *Sleeping with Dogs and Other Lovers,* sparks fly as matchmaker extraordinaire Cynthia Amas tries to make sense of her own increasingly complicated -- and steamy -- love life."
— *Kindle Nation*

www.TruLoveStories.com
Where Passionistas Play!

BroadLit

January 2013

Published by

BroadLit ®
14011 Ventura Blvd.
Suite 206 E
Sherman Oaks, CA 91423

ISBN 978-0-9887627-5-6

Produced in the United States of America.

To all the women, like me, who are taking a second chance at love, life and new ventures.

I would like to thank first and always, Barbara Weller, Cynthia Cleveland and Nancy Cushing-Jones, who are not only the inspiration for this story, but also my dedicated and crazy but brilliant editors and the best girlfriends ever. I also want to thank my husband, Dilbert, whose nightly visits to the neighborhood donut shop sustained me throughout those long nights burning the midnight oil at my computer.

HEARTS UNLEASHED

A SECOND
ACTS NOVEL

by JULIA DUMONT

A BROADLIT BOOK

Chapter 1

SATURDAY AFTERNOON

Three fingertips caressed Cynthia's trembling lips as five others traveled slowly from hip to thigh. The hot late-morning sun was the least of what was warming her now. "Oh, Pete..." she whispered softly, gazing at an expanse of blue, framed by gently swaying palms.

Breathing together, gaining momentum, Pete felt the sting of perspiration and sunblock in his eyes. "Cynthia," he sighed, smiling, but his mouth barely open, "we can't... go on meeting like this."

She gasped and laughed a little, but that didn't impede her descent into that brief moment of stillness she always arrived at just before climax, holding her breath, clinging to those two or three seconds of order before all control slipped away. 3...2...1... "Oh, god," she cried out, shoulders compressing, fingers trembling, her entire body spasming as she sank deep into the cushion, bracing herself with one hand to avoid melting off the couch and onto the floor.

"Cynthia!" cried Pete, "You're out of frame!" She quickly moved in closer, giving her lover a better look at her face, her neck, her breasts. And then he finished too, falling back onto the bed, his legs swinging upward, his toes pointing like a dancer's.

He was in his hotel room overlooking breathtaking Balekambang Beach in East Java and she was in her living room in Los Angeles. They shared passions, compliments of FaceTime via the iPad propped on her coffee table and his phone, clutched tightly with his free hand. Cynthia had sometimes only been looking at parts of his thumb and fingers.

But visuals are not nearly as necessary for women at such moments. They have better imaginations. And visual recall. Cynthia knew the exact color of Pete's eyes, the contour of his lips, the perfect imperfections of his face.

"I swear," she said, pushing her hair off of her forehead, "if it weren't for this 4G network, you would completely forget what I look like."

"That's ridiculous," he said, rolling over onto his side and staring at the phone.

"Okay," she said, first kissing the screen and then turning the iPad around, giving Pete a view of the coffee table and the dining room in the distance, "how many freckles do I have on my face?"

"Oh, that's easy," said Pete, "and a trick question, because, my dear, you have no freckles anywhere."

Cynthia felt disappointed and vindicated at the same time. She didn't say a word. She just stood up and proceeded to take Pete on a tour. She pulled the screen in close, aiming as best she could at the bridge of her nose.

"Welcome aboard the Freckle Bus. If you look out the window to your left, you'll see a sweet cluster of delicate specimens, right there on the main thoroughfare. What's that, sir? Why yes, that's true, this little enclave is literally as plain as the nose on my face."

"Oh, right," said Pete. "*Those* freckles. Well, yeah, obviously. I was merely saying that you don't have any freckles *besides* those freckles."

"Okay, everybody," said Cynthia to imaginary tourist-passengers, putting on a megaphone-like voice straight out of vaudeville, and moving the iPad down her body, making a small-car putt-putting noise. "Next stop, Titty City," she announced, pushing in tight to her left nipple, making a soft squealing-brake sound and there, to Pete's utter surprise, were three tiny freckles nestled sweetly near her areola. "This," she said, "is known as the Maliboob Colony, an exclusive dominion reserved for only the most exclusive Hollywood denizens of the melanin pigment variety."

"Wow," said Pete. "I have to admit I missed those too."

"Right," she replied, moving the iPad downward to her belly button and stopping there. "Would you like this tour of shame to continue? Next stop, Upper Thighville."

"Oh, if I have to," said Pete, now totally on board, the embarrassment over his less than stellar powers of observation gladly giving way to his deep interest in the subject matter.

As for Cynthia, she realized that her style of FaceTime seduction was directly indebted to her ex-boyfriend Max Ramsey and his remarkably creative methods of long-distance foreplay. But she didn't care...she was making it her own with Pete. Perhaps this was Max's one enduring legacy.

She was also feeling inspired by the challenge. Cynthia and Pete were beginners in the realm of phone romance, not to mention any kind of romance with each other, having just resumed dating after a very long hiatus—actually since high school when they were each other's first crushes. The whole thing was sort of crazy. She had planned on joining Pete somewhere on the Asian leg of his music tour with his band, but it hadn't worked out. Opening Second Acts Dating Service's new office in Los Feliz, just down the hill from her residence in Runyon Canyon, blocks away from the Hollywood sign, had turned out to be even more demanding of her time than she'd imagined. For one thing, she had hired a new assistant who decided to quit and run off with her boyfriend after three weeks, so now she faced training her *new* new assistant——Paloma Rodriguez, a beautiful, young U.C.L.A. graduate who had deep roots in L.A. and was almost positively going to stick around. She was an aspiring actress, so although there was a chance that she'd snag a career-transforming role, Cynthia was pretty sure she'd be a reliable employee for at least a year or two, which was about as much one could hope for in star-struck Los Angeles.

But back to the matter of the challenge of multiple go-rounds. It seemed almost unthinkable. There was a level of silliness about the whole thing. It felt a little cold and futuristic, staring into an electronic facsimile of the object of one's lust. That said, once you went with it, really *went* with it, it was surprisingly erotic.

"Okay, big boy," she whispered, "come with me." She was completely aware of her double entendre.

She moved the iPad back upward, turning it sideways, filling the entire screen, and framing her breasts like a work of art. She reached down with the other hand, and brought back a sliver of ice between her index and middle fingers from her water glass on the coffee table. She fondled one breast, then the other.

Pete moved his phone in close to his face, making her wet erect nipples larger than life, like he was in the front row of an Imax theater. He exhaled, fogging the screen slightly.

From time to time throughout this "conversation," notices popped up on the top of Cynthia's screen: *You have 23 new notifications on Facebook. You have eleven new emails. Sig Alert on the 405. Congress filibusters jobs bill again.* She was very good at blocking all this out in order to concentrate on Pete. But one particular text message caught her eye. Well, rather it was the *sender* of the message: one Ava Dodd Radcliffe. And there really could only be one of those. Radcliffe was a well-known, incredibly rich, relatively young, recently widowed ex-actress. She had married Jonathon Radcliffe, the movie-TV-internet-oh-let's-face-it-*everything* mogul, when she was *incredibly* young, and dropped out of acting, a la Grace Kelly. And then, about two years ago, Jonathon died of a massive heart attack while hang-gliding off Bixby Bridge on Route 1 in Big Sur. Ava had leaped off right behind him and didn't know until about halfway down——when her trajectory happened to afford her a clear view of his limp body dangling like a marionette——that he had in fact expired. The stunning natural beauty of the site——soaring arcs of the bridge's buttresses, rugged cliffs laced with green, the breathtaking beach and surf below——made the horrible tragedy that much more shocking, heartbreaking... beyond operatic.

Why on Earth is Ava Dodd Radcliffe texting me?

Meanwhile, Cynthia had forgotten all about Pete, who suddenly cried out with pleasure, falling back onto the bed and losing his grip on the phone, which flew across the room, striking something hard——wall, ceiling, headboard?—— with a loud crack.

Whatever it was, it transformed his smart phone into a deaf, dumb, and blind phone, and caused Cynthia's iPad to go black.

Cynthia burst into laughter. Merely one of the hazards of long-distance romance, she supposed. She pictured Pete in post-orgasmic stupor crawling around looking for the runaway device and wished more than ever she was there with him. Her phone buzzed: Pete calling from the hotel phone. She answered.

"Was it as good for you as it sounded?" she asked with a smile in her voice.

"Cynthia. Would you please get on a plane and get the hell over here?"

Here we go again she thought.

"Why don't you come *here*?"

"You know I would if I could. We have twenty-one concerts in the next twenty-five days. There's literally not enough of a break in there to even *get* to L.A. and back... *without* pausing for a quickie with you on the tarmac. Can't you just take off two or three days? Can't you do almost everything via email and phone anyway?"

Cynthia was a bit irritated by this.

"Pete...we've been over this. No, I can't. I just opened the place. The whole point is that my service is personal."

"Yeah," said Pete, "well, it would be nice if what we've been doing for the last two months was just a tad more personal too."

He was obviously right.

"I know, sweetie...but..." she said, immediately realizing she had nothing to follow that "but" with that either or both of them hadn't already said at least once over the past weeks. It was one of those uncomfortable phone silences that occur when neither party can find words to express the upside of a situation that clearly had no upside.

"Okay," said Pete, pulling on shorts and shirt, "well, I guess I might as well see if there's an Apple store nearby. See if they can hook me up with another of their kinky sex toys."

They both laughed now.

"Maybe while you're there you should pick up an iPad too. I recommend it."

"Yeah, you're right. Maybe I'll do that. I'll call you tonight after the show. I trust you will be ready for your close-up?"

"Ready and willing, Mr. DeMille," she smiled, loving that their cultural points of reference were so in tune so much of the time. And again wishing they could be together. She had dated a younger guy a few years back who didn't know that Sunset Boulevard wasn't just a street.

"Okay, see you later then," he said.

"Bye, bye, baby," she replied, clicking off. She felt a pang of sadness about their situation. She really adored him. Except for the absurd geographic dilemma and all the problems that presented, they couldn't be better suited for each other.

Chapter 2

SATURDAY AFTERNOON

But back to Ava Dodd Radcliffe. Cynthia re-read her message.

"Dear Miss Amas...I admire what you're doing with 2nd Acts. I have a proposal. Perhaps we might meet at your earliest convenience?"

Perhaps we might meet at your earliest convenience. Sheeven *texted* wealthy.

Cynthia thought about Ava Radcliffe's situation. Aside from the occasional notice in the news about her appearances at dry fundraisers for one of the many cultural institutions on whose board she sat, there had been no indication that she was back in the dating market. At all. Judging from published group photos, she still seemed gripped by an overwhelming sadness that even vast worldly riches had no discernable effect upon. It was understandable. She had married Jonathon, more than twenty years her senior, when she was barely out of college. And although she'd had a short but lucrative modeling career in her teens and a few early plum roles in film, including *True Love Lost*, for which she had been nominated for an Oscar and broken the hearts of millions of teenage boys, she immediately abandoned all work within months of her wedding day. As in most such cases, people speculated about whether their plan was to quickly start a family. But no babies arrived, which of course instead bred more speculation. As time went on, it appeared that they were just deeply in love and loved being together almost all of the time...traveling, sailing, polo-playing, mountain climbing, all kind of rich-people activities, including, yes, tragically, hang-gliding.

Cynthia had always been intrigued by Ava Dodd Radcliffe as a public figure. She was indisputably a true beauty, but she also radiated intelligence and talent. In addition to acting, she was an accomplished artist, a painter...another passion lost through the miracle of matrimony. Cynthia had wondered, long before Jonathon died, if Ava might have been possessed with some level of sadness and regret over the choice to turn her back on her personal dreams and goals, however blissful the marriage appeared from the outside. All that was moot now, of course. Her sadness was now the very first thing one noticed about her.

Cynthia looked back at the text.

"I have a proposal."

At first Cynthia had taken that sentence to mean simply the proposal that they'd meet. But when she looked at it again, it occurred to her that maybe she meant a business proposal. Did she want to be partners in Second Acts? Did she want to buy the company outright? Or was it some other separate business idea? If Cynthia's memory served, the Radcliffe fortune was somewhere in the neighborhood of a billion dollars. In that neighborhood why go looking for headaches? On the other hand, if Ava had merely decided to become a Second Acts *client*, why characterize that as a proposal?

Only one way to find out, she thought. She wasn't sure about the etiquette.

Hi Ms. Radcliffe.

Wait, she had called Cynthia "Miss." Nobody had called her that since the 1980's...since way before she'd been married and divorced. Cynthia had been using "Ms." for so long it no longer occurred to her to use anything else. Until now. But "Miss" was even less appropriate for Ava than for herself. And "Mrs." seemed so old-fashioned. But maybe billionaires, even relatively young ones, are old fashioned.

Hi, Ava, maybe? Too familiar.

Hi, Ava Dodd Radcliffe? Verbose.

Keep it simple. Texts should be brief.

Hi. Would love to. Lunch? Thursday or Friday? Happy to come to you. Let me know where/when. Thanks.

Wait. *"Lunch"* is too presumptuous. Make it *"coffee."* Okay, good. Send.

Now just wait.

Cynthia got up and walked toward the kitchen. Halfway there, the phone bleeped: Ava Dodd Radcliffe.

Wow, this is one anxious billionaire.

Chapter 3

Max Ramsey stepped out of the ornate hotel lobby and into the pounding Dublin rain. A doorman held an umbrella for him, but this was the kind of downpour that laughs at umbrellas. He was soaked by the time he boarded the first cab in line. He usually liked rainy Dublin autumns, but for the past eight days, he had not seen so much as a sliver of sun. He'd been doing quite a bit of California daydreaming in response. Even though this had been a momentous trip. Or at least potentially momentous. He'd spent the past two weeks working on a merger deal for the Irish tech company he had co-founded years earlier and that had recently gone through the roof. This was a big deal, one that could change the lives of everyone involved.

But with Max, no trip was all business. Emily, a lovely young woman from Cork, who the company had assigned to Max as his assistant and tour guide, emerged from the lobby with her own umbrella and slid onto the seat beside him. Immediately, even before he directed the Irish cabbie as to what their destination would be, he gently pulled aside the drenched hair from her face and kissed her. The cabbie no doubt concluded that they were deeply in love. But the truth was that even though Max had jumped into bed with Emily exactly two hours after she'd picked him up at the airport thirteen days earlier, now he was already thinking about Lolita. And Cyn. Together. There's a thought. He wasn't so deluded to think that could possibly happen. He just loved thinking about it.

Max said, "Dublin International," and then took out his phone and speed-dialed Lolita.

Emily kissed his neck and slid her hand between his thighs, coming to a halt at his balls, cupping them firmly through his trousers for a few moments before continuing slowly up along the length of his shaft and unzipping his fly.

"Max," answered Lolita, not surprised in the least to hear from him, since he had been calling her more than once a day, "hold on just a minute. I'm with a client." By client, she meant a seven-pound toy Yorky with a ribbon in its hair and a real diamond-and-pearl necklace/collar that was worth more than Lolita's car. A lot more, actually. She handed the dog over to its two-hundred-and-forty pound "Mommy," who was wearing an identical necklace and signing the credit card printout, adding a fifteen-percent tip onto the $1,200.00 charge.

Max stared out the window at the rain as Emily started doing something with the tip of her tongue that was unlike anything he had ever felt. He honestly wasn't sure *what* she was doing down there. Just then, Lolita rejoined the conversation.

"So, Max, you must be on the way to the airport by now."

Max's head was leaning way back. His mouth was wide open and his arm had dropped, taking the phone far from his mouth. He was in a state of stunned arousal, unable to move.

"Emily, Emily, Emily..." he whispered.

"Emily?" asked Lolita. "Max? Are you there? Who's Emily?" Although totally aware of Max's womanizing ways, she had little inkling of the staggering depths of his deception. She never would have guessed that the same man who had pined over her for days in a row now, who had repeatedly declared his love for her, and had persuaded her to meet him at LAX very, very early the next morning, could possibly have the gall to call her while receiving world class felatio from a "work associate" half a world away.

Max struggled to sound coherent. "Emily is a little dog who belongs to someone at the hotel. A little Pug. Adorable."

"Aww..." said Lolita, obviously a sucker for any dog anytime.

Emily squeezed Max's buttocks just hard enough to register her objection.

"Ahhh!" he blurted.

Emily giggled and got back to work.

The cabbie rolled his eyes and shook his head. He hated working in the rain anyway, but he especially hated people who fooled around on his backseat.

Then Emily did something with her fingers and her lips and god only knew what else that almost sent Max through the roof of the cab.

Max inhaled sharply and somehow recovered enough to raise the phone back up to the vicinity of his face, muttering something about *bad reception and I'm losing you and I may have to reschedule my flight and I'll call you soon and I'm losing you and…Hello? Hello? Okay, good-bye, and all that.*

The cabbie was steaming now. He was generally bitter about his own life and certain kinds of behavior from certain kinds of people could quickly bring his blood and bitterness to a boil.

"Okay, then," said Lolita. "Let me know. All that to you too."

Emily administered one last bit of alchemy down below, causing Max to utter one last "EMILY!!!!!" while kicking involuntarily into the back of the driver's seat, thrusting the cabbie forward against the horn, blaring a sharp warning to the elderly nun crossing at the crosswalk in front of them, who jumped about a foot in the air and stared daggers at the driver.

"God damn you!" barked the cabbie, his head still straight ahead, so that it appeared to the nun that his remark was directed at her.

"Jesus Christ Almighty!" she shrieked, turning toward the car. "Isn't it bad enough that I'm drenched to the bone from the devil's own monsoon for Christ's sake?" She peered in through the windshield.

"Seamus O'Brien, is that you?" she asked incredulously. "Haven't you matured one iota since your expulsion from

St. Michael's?" This nun had wrapped the cabbie's knuckles on a regular basis in the seventh grade. "I'm going to tell your mother you're spending your waking hours terrorizing ninety- year-old nuns with your bloody horn!"

Emily looked up at Max. "You're welcome to terrorize me with your horn any day."

This was too much for the cabbie. As soon as the light turned green, he pulled over.

"Get out of my fucking cab, you fuckin' ugly American and, Emily, you poor wayward lass!"

Max and Emily spilled onto the sidewalk and giggled, splashing through puddles like school kids, all the way back to the hotel. Max called the airline and while waiting on hold, he proceeded to peel every drenched garment off Emily's lithe body and feast upon her loins, already slippery from rain and anticipation, but getting slipperier and more delicious by the minute.

The hotel maid, thinking Max had finally checked out, tiptoed out of the bathroom and almost to the door before he spotted her and, turning momentarily from his work and flashing his famous megawatt smile, asked if she wanted to join them. Emily laughed out loud at his joke——even as Max's tongue dived back deep inside, then out and around, fluttering mercilessly at her "good spot" as she called it. But he wasn't kidding. Max would have claimed it was a joke under interrogation, but it most certainly was not. Unfortunately for Emily, she was even more deluded than Lolita. She had only known Max for a short time.

The maid screamed and left.

Emily screamed louder and came.

Chapter 4

SUNDAY AM

Four blocks away, right in front of the Brendan Behan statue on Upper Dorset Street, Seamus O'Brien dropped off another fare. As the passenger opened the door, she stopped and picked something up.

"Some poor American forgot these items back here," she said handing Seamus a business card, an American Express card, and a Starbucks card.

"Oh, thank you," said Seamus as the lady stepped onto the street and slammed the door. "You don't need to be slammin' it!" he said for approximately the three-thousandth time in his cabbie career. He shook his head and tucked all three items into his wallet. Then he gazed up at the Brendan

Behan statue, the first bit of sun in days moving from behind clouds and providing dramatic backlighting for the great Irish playwright, poet, novelist, and infamous drinker. Behan was one of the cabbie's heroes. He'd made a splash across the pond way back in the 1950's and O'Brien had always wanted to follow in his footsteps. Leaving out the prison stints and the whole horrible-death-by-drinking thing, of course. Seamus had a mountain of short stories, any one of which would make a far better major motion picture than ninety percent of the crap out there, and he was beyond sick and tired of driving a fucking cab. He also had an older brother who owned a coffee shop in Hollywood. Seamus wasn't tied down. No wife. No kids. Just a twelve-year-old beagle named Samuel Beckett and the fourteen-year-old piece of shite taxi that had become his prison on wheels. It was time for a change. He pulled over, out of traffic, and called Donald Griffin O'Brien.

"O'Brien's Irish café, dart coliseum, and musical emporium... what can I get you for?"

"Brother Donald," said Seamus with more enthusiasm than he'd expressed in the last ten years, "I'm comin' your way. It's high time for me to conquer the United States of America."

"Hallelujah," said Donald. "It's about feckin time. I've got to introduce you to my girl, Adriana. And our friend Cynthia Amas, the genius matchmaker to the stars." He looked at Cynthia, who happened to be sitting right there. "He's handsomer than me, myself, and I rolled into one. He wants to be a writer, but he's a born movie star. I think you'd like him."

"I'm not in the market," smiled Cynthia.

"Anyone whose booty call is brought to her courtesy of a handheld device is in the market," said Adriana, rubbing Cynthia's shoulders like she was preparing a prizefighter for a championship bout.

"Okay then," said Donald into the phone, "we'll see you when you get here. I've got a couch with your name on it."

Seamus drove home, packed a suitcase with more notebooks than clothes, put Samuel Beckett into his carrier, and headed for his nephew's house.

"Matt, my boy," he said with a smile, when the nephew appeared at the door in his underwear. Matt had lost his job as a bouncer at a local pub six months earlier. "What exactly did I give you for your birthday last year?"

"Umm...well, Uncle Seamus," he mumbled, wiping the sleep out of his eyes, "I'm not sure you gave me exactly *anything*."

"Well, happy birthday, then," said Seamus, handing him the keys to the cab. "The title is in the glove box. The tires are new. I can't account for the rest of the piece of shite, but it does run. Or at least limps relatively quickly. For now."

"Uncle Seamus," he said beaming, "I do not know what to say."

"How about, 'Certainly, Uncle Seamus, I'd be pleased as St. Patrick on a mountain of dead serpents to drive you to the bloody airport.'"

Chapter 5

MONDAY AM

Cynthia woke up and before she even opened her eyes, she remembered that she needed to get back to her blog. She had started writing a dating advice column for her website and had been overwhelmed with letters in the past few weeks. Writing it was fun. It was finding the time to write that was difficult. She would just have to stop what she was doing and do it. One letter seemed to almost jump right out at her.

Dear Second Acts;

I met a guy while on vacation at a resort last year. I really like almost everything about him. Except he travels all the time. At first it seemed like we could cope with it…that I could go along with him sometimes, talk on the phone a lot, just deal, you know? But the reality of the situation is far from workable. Most of the time I'm too busy with my job to go meet up with him. On the rare occasion that I do, he's too busy to take time off and I end up hanging around at the hotel, wishing I'd stayed home. But, get this: I have fallen in love with this guy and I can't seem to stop loving him.

Please help,

Stranded in Louisiana

Dear Stranded;

You will never know just how deeply I feel your pain. Years ago I was in a somewhat similar situation. The cold hard, ironic truth is that long distance relationships cannot last long. The sooner you face this, the better off you'll be.

Cynthia stopped typing for a moment and stared out the window. This letter was ridiculously close to the bone. "Years ago," what a joke.

Anyway, Stranded. If you feel that you can trust your boyfriend, and that's a big if, you need to at least put a time limit

on this long-distance madness. Talk to him and tell him how you feel. Together agree on an end date. Dating a musician is never easy and you can't allow it to go forever like this.
Yours,
Second Acts

Cynthia looked over what she'd written and shook her head. Stranded never said anything about her man being a musician. Cynthia changed it to "Dating *anyone* long distance is never easy..."

She hated the expression OMG but she said OMG out loud, involuntarily.

A few hours later, Cynthia was moving west on Wilshire, passing into the Miracle Mile district, when her phone buzzed. It was her best friend Lolita, who also happened to be one of Cynthia's first and most challenging Second Acts clients. Despite her claims to the contrary, she was more in the market for lust than love.

"Hi, Sweetie," she answered, "Miss you."

"Yeah, you're telling me," said Lolita. "I haven't even seen your new place all finished. Are you trying to avoid me?"

"No, no...why don't you come by tomorrow morning and we can grab a bite of breakfast in the neighborhood."

"Well, no," she said. "I can't tomorrow. I have to go down to the airport super early."

"Leaving town?" asked Cynthia. Lolita hardly ever went away. She was as married to her business as Cynthia was to hers.

"Not a chance," said Lolita. "I'm picking someone up."

"Which someone is that?"

"Ahh...nobody special. Not important."

Cynthia knew Lolita well. She would only make a super early airport run for a guy. And she was not shy about offering details about guys...the who, what, where, why of them. So it was obvious to her that this was a guy whose identity she was trying to keep secret. Which could only mean one guy. She knew why Lolita wanted to keep it from her, even though she really didn't care. It was more of an issue of embarrassment. Max was one of the guiltiest pleasures in the world.

"So," said Cynthia in the deadest of deadpans, "you're picking up Max at the airport then."

After a five second pause that seemed a lot longer, Lolita burst into laughter and Cynthia followed suit. It was the kind of hearty, crying laughter that makes driving dangerous. Cynthia needed to make a concerted effort to not crash the car.

Max Ramsey figured prominently in both of their histories. He had been Cynthia's longtime, on-again, off-again, highly desirable object of desire. He was one indisputable hunk of tall, dark, and handsome and a true master of the carnal arts. He was hilarious and intelligent and his love of life and mischievous sense of adventure were intoxicating and infectious. He was a dream lover in many ways. Unfortunately, he also happened to be one of the great womanizers of the western world. He had an irrepressible lust for lust. He aimed to please and be pleased. And even though he was quite direct about his proudly professed non-monogamy, Cynthia had always been quite aware that the schedule of sexual extracurriculars in his well-worn datebook was far more rich and varied than she would ever know. Cynthia and Max were no more.

Lolita and Max had just begun. It was as if he'd been passed along from one friend to another, almost like a good book...a good book with great benefits. Most friendships could never withstand this sort of incestuous cross-pollination. The fact that Cynthia and Lolita seemed to be taking it in stride was a testament to their deep affection for one another. It was also made possible by several facts. One, Cynthia was over, truly over Max. It had taken years, but she finally knew that he would never change and that she would never stop wanting him to. She would always cherish her memories of their time together, but had absolutely no intension of acquiring more. And two, Lolita had just met Max. So, for one thing, the fruit of his loins was still ripe, still fresh, still irresistible. Also, since Lolita was not really looking for much more than great, endless rolls in the hay, she had no illusions nor unrealistic expectations. In this way, they were a match made in heaven. Some kind of wild, hedonistic version of heaven. But it was not just the sex. He made her laugh.

And so did Cynthia. They really hadn't known each other terribly long, but they'd grown incredibly close. They got each other. The fact that Cynthia was still supposedly looking for a match for Lolita was totally beside the point. In some ways it was merely a ruse to spend even more time together. They both had friends they'd known much longer, but for now anyway, none came close in terms of real-life day-to-day quality and quantity contact. They were textbook examples of fast friends. On paper, it would be almost inexplicable, but yet here they were, two people not in the market for BFFs, but now unable to imagine life without the other.

They laughed for six full blocks of Wilshire, before Cynthia pulled into the parking structure of the Los Angeles County

Museum of Art.

"Listen, Lo," she said, wiping a tear from her eye and taking the ticket from the machine, "I gotta go. I'm parking."

"Where are you going on this fine Monday morning?"

"I'm at LACMA. I'm meeting——get this——Ava Dodd Radcliffe for breakfast. So, I've really gotta get..."

"Hold on! You don't gotta *nada*! Except explain. But wait. I hate to break it to you...LACMA isn't even *open* on Mondays. I think you've got your wires crossed."

Cynthia locked the car with a beep and headed toward the museum's side entrance. "Hate to break it to *you*, but they're opening just for us. Well, for her. She wanted to meet me, to show me some new exhibit, and apparently she's bringing along her private chef. I guess it's just one of the perks of donating twenty million dollars to a major cultural institution."

"Oh, right. Why didn't I think of that? Okay, smuggle out some crumbs for me and the other riff-raff. Please trickle down, Little Miss One Percent. But wait. Wait. What's this meeting about?"

"No idea. I don't even know what the exhibit is. Gotta go."

Chapter 6

Cynthia passed through the oversized doorway, where a museum guard greeted and escorted her to her destination. The echo of their footsteps was unbelievably loud as they moved through empty cavernous corridors, passing gallery after gallery.

The guard turned left and, walking on a large white tarp——the exhibition was clearly still in the process of being installed——pulled apart a floor-to-ceiling red velvet curtain, revealing two oversized steel orbs, probably eighteen or twenty feet tall, painted to resemble gigantic breasts. The effect was startling and funny. The fronts were sensitively, nearly photo-realistically rendered to replicate the warmth and softness of flesh. But the opposite sides were unpainted, rusted metal, giving the impression of some kind of massive ocean buoys or water mines. They weren't unlike the huge breast balloon from the Woody Allen movie *Everything You Always Wanted to Know About Sex *But Were Afraid to Ask,* except they were not balloons. On the contrary, they looked to Cynthia like they probably weighed a ton each. These were monumental mammaries...simultaneously formidable, indestructible, tender, and sexy.

As they passed through the curved triangular opening formed by the intersection of colossal boobs and floor, Cynthia looked up and had the sense of being in an x-rated production of *Gulliver's Travels, The Incredible Shrinking Man, or Attack of the 50-Foot Woman.*

And then she saw the rest of the room: an exhibition of erotic art throughout history. There were Incan pots, Greek statues, Japanese prints, Picasso paintings, Egon Schiele nudes, erotic illustrations, "abstract" work that really was not abstract in the slightest, all depicting intercourse, oral sex, every style of sex, in every imaginable position and pre or post-coital situation. Tons of nude photography too...from Edward Weston to Mapplethorpe to Helmut Newton. It was an amazing display. It was like mainlining a potent hit of erotic fantasy just being in there.

The guard appeared a bit embarrassed. "Miss Amas," he said, pointing to a small, elegant table with two chairs in the middle of the room, "if you would, please have a seat. Miss Radcliffe will be with you shortly."

Cynthia sat down and continued to drink in the sights. There was a small painting depicting a satyr with a tree-limb-like erection about three times the length of his body and a beautiful fox-faced woman tickling its tip with a peacock feather. All manner of woodland creatures were perched upon or dangling from it, all with devilish expressions of euphoria and sexual mischief. It had an early Renaissance feel. Cynthia thought maybe it had been painted by someone like Pieter Brueghel or Hieronymus Bosch during the 15th century. She stared at it, mesmerized.

"Hello, Cynthia. I see you're a Petra Von Reudenhoff fan?"

"A Petra Von Who-inhoff?" asked Cynthia, turning around to see Ava Dodd Radcliffe standing before her. "Oh, the painting," she continued, "I guess I didn't know I was a fan until just now."

Cynthia stood up and they shook hands. Ava's face was much more beautiful in person. She had the kind of lustrous complexion that cannot be captured by photography or faked with make-up. It was as if her bone structure, skin, and blood flow all conspired to create a radiance that was far, far more than simply the sum of its parts. She was dressed in the kind of loose, lightweight, casual clothing that is so simple, at first glance it seems inexpensive. But the closer you look the more you realize it is incredibly well made...impeccable design and construction. It seemed effortless. This particular ensemble was probably five thousand dollars worth of effortlessness.

"Don't worry," Ava said with a small, but thoroughly charming smile, "I just discovered Petra myself a few months ago. I curated this show. It's the first major exhibit of erotic art in a major American museum."

"I've certainly never seen anything like it," said Cynthia, surveying the contents of the room again. "Certainly stimulating."

"I know," said Ava. "It's hard to think about anything else when you're in here. But I'm hungry for actual food too... let's eat." They sat down. "Sutherland?" Ava called softly, glancing over at a short handsome man in a black suit and white apron, who was standing in the far corner of the room. Sutherland disappeared. "Sutherland is wonderful. He's been with me for years. He traveled all over the world with

Jonathon and me. Very devoted. And a superb chef."

Sutherland appeared again and served food, wine, more food, and more wine. It was incredibly delicious, but Cynthia barely tasted it because as soon as Ava launched into explaining why they were there, all other concerns were trumped.

"As you may know, Cynthia, I married Jonathon Radcliffe when I was young. *Incredibly* young. I was so in love. It never even occurred to me I'd live without him. I mean he was a lot older, but still, I guess I was in denial about that. And I certainly didn't think he'd die at sixty-four. I was planning on at least twenty more years. Anyway, I've been quite numb for the past two years. I sit on the boards of some corporations... plus this place, the symphony, and lots of other cultural institutions. So I sort of increased my involvement with all that, you know, to keep busy.

"Anyway, Jonathon and I had collected art for a long time and a portion of it was of an overtly sexual nature. It started when I became interested in the Leda and Swan myth...the story of how Zeus took the form of a swan and seduced, some say raped, Leda...the mother of Helen of Troy. Many, many artists have depicted Leda and the Swan throughout art history——from the Greeks, the Romans, in sculptures and mosaics, to the Renaissance, DaVinci, Michelangelo, and all the way to modern day. There are many beautiful versions and I own a couple of the very best: Peter Paul Rubens, as a student, painted a copy of a Michelangelo, which itself did not survive. But the Rubens, which hung over our bed for fifteen years, is right over there."

Cynthia turned and saw the painting in question. She had noticed it when she walked in, but now it took on a warm glow and presence that was undoubtedly enhanced by Ava's story and the painting's history. It was truly gorgeous. Leda and the large swan were entangled in the act, her lips and his bill kissing delicately, their gazes fixed upon each other's eyes. It was undeniably erotic, but also surreal. How many women fantasize about making love with a large water foul? And yet, the beauty of the painting——the stunning arrangement of red-orange bedding, brown and white feathers, and peachy flesh, together with the perfectly composed, choreographed positions of this highly unlikely couple——made one believe it. You could totally buy that it might happen, that it might be, well...good. Ava and Jonathon had not only "bought" it, they'd *literally* bought it.

"It is incredible," said Cynthia.

"I know. And, well, what happened was this. When

Jonathon died, I didn't want to sleep in our bedroom. I tried sleeping in every other room in the house, but I couldn't. I literally could not fall asleep for a month. Never more than a catnap here and therethroughout the day. Finally, I moved to our house in Hawaii, but that was no better. I tried the place we have in the South of France...outside of Nice. Nothing. This was becoming a worldwide bout with insomnia. The Guinness people should probably have been notified. But finally, I returned here, to the Brentwood house. I arrived at around eleven in the morning and, despite the fact that it seemed completely wrong, I was drawn back to the master bedroom for the first time. I walked in and looked up at Leda and the Swan. I own a lot of houses but that painting felt more like home than anything else in my life. I wished I could be *in* the painting. An incredible rush of emotion came over me and I collapsed, weeping, upon the bed. I slept for three solid days. And I had some very strange dreams."

"Wow," said Cynthia. She realized that she had been frozen with her mouth open, a forkful of linguini dangling in front of her face.

"Please," smiled Ava, "have a bite. I'll pause."

Cynthia was a little embarrassed. She quickly chewed, swallowed, and put the fork down.

"Anyway," Ava continued, "I don't want to bore you by recounting dreams. I hate when people do that." She took her first sip of red wine. Then another. One more. Her lovely lips were slightly stained by the cabernet.

"Ava, I really don't think I would be bored. At all."

Ava smiled. The naturally rosiness of her cheeks intensified by twenty or so percentage points. She opened her mouth to speak, but stopped herself with two fingers to her lips. She closed her eyes for a moment and opened them again.

"I've missed him so much," she said. "Even the boring stuff, the homey stuff. Eating breakfast, taking baths together. I might miss that the most. In a weird way, there's no greater comfort than in sharing the mundane."

"I know," said Cynthia, "I agree." She was thinking about Pete and how they hadn't had the chance to get to the point where sublime moments like that occur.

Cynthia suddenly realized that Ava's eyes had welled up. Attempting to speak at moments like that can be like the turn of a faucet. "Oh, my," said Cynthia, "no need to continue." She thought about getting up to hug her or touch her shoulder...to comfort her somehow, but it seemed way too familiar. She instead simply reached across the table and put her hand, palm down, within reach, if Ava chose to do so.

And she did. She put her hand on top of Cynthia's.

"Thanks," she said. "This is turning into quite the lunch."

She was right. The grand scale of the museum gallery, the erotic intensity of the roomful of art, the beautiful young bride giving up her career, the death-by-hang-gliding, and all of that, rendered the entire experience cinematic, almost overwhelming. Cynthia was deeply touched by the whole thing. In fact, she felt it was entirely possible that if Ava did burst into tears, she might very well follow suit.

"Anyway," said Ava, patting Cynthia's hand and then reaching for the bottle of wine and filling both glasses, "suffice it to say that the dream——really a series of dreams over those days——was life-changing. I woke up knowing three things. One, I wanted to curate a show like this; two, I wanted to start painting again; and three, I wanted to start dating."

"So, wait. That's when you called me?"

"Well, no. Not immediately anyway. I made it known that I was interested in getting out of the house. There was a lot of interest...but mostly from the withered and wealthy. Apparently, everybody assumed that since Jonathon was older, I'd obviously want someone his age. I wasn't necessarily against that. But out-living another husband wasn't exactly a priority either. In any case, every unmarried, filthy-rich codger on Earth came knocking on my door. But every one of them left me cold. They all seemed like cheap imitations of Jonathon. And even the *younger* ones seemed dull. They wanted marriage, but obviously had a much greater passion for money——theirs or mine——than they'd ever have for anything else...including me.

"Look, I don't even know if I *want* to get married again. I did that at age twenty-one. Now I want...let's just say, *more*."

She paused and took another large sip of wine, licked her lips, and continued.

"In short, Cynthia," Ava Dodd Radcliffe whispered, "I am sick of who I am. I'm sick and *tired* of being the good girl. I've had just about enough of this particular version of me. I'm going to be direct. Let's face it; I could simply *pay* for it. Plenty of wealthy widows do. But I adore meaningful relationships. I care far too much about interesting people... their thoughts, their talents, and their ideas. So why not choose interesting people who also happen to be *beautiful*? And why not make them able to make me *laugh* while they're making me squeal, for instance? Is that too much to ask? And why limit it to *men*? I want to know *more*. And *feel* more. A *lot* more. And why only one man or woman at a time? I don't know, I'm just asking. Don't get me wrong, I loved my husband dearly, but since I can't bring him back to life, why not seek adventure? If I find the right one, so be it, but why not at least make the process, the journey, *stimulating*? In every sense of the word.

"So, that brings me to you. Actually," she said giggling slightly, seeming a little tipsy now, "that brings *you* to *me*. The proposal I was talking about. What about you finding me an evolving crew of scintillating conversationalists for dinner parties——maybe for group vacations, retreats, and so on——all of whom would be open to loving relationships... and, most importantly, extremely interesting connections. And at least for the first encounter, all total strangers to each other and me. These could be Second Acts events... we would sort of be working together in that way, but I don't want any money for it...I'll be paying *you*. You'd get the use of my various homes and locations...believe me, we're talking a lot of pretty cool spots. If other people pair off, that's fine. I'm not looking for orgies or anything...just a good time where I can meet a lot of interesting people. Yes, I want romance, but many of these people would simply become part of my social circle, you know? I desperately want some fresh blood in my life. I'm tired of old blood...old blue blood especially. My husband is gone and my many obscenely large homes scattered around the globe are devastatingly empty. I mean...dusty, echo-filled castles of sadness. In the two years since Jonathon passed, I've received no less than thirty-seven marriage proposals. And they're all nice guys. But, I don't know...marrying any of them feels like marrying death. In the short term, I'd rather go steady with *life*. If I'm emotionally capable of it that is." Her voice cracked. "I'm totally aware that this is a big job, but I'll pay you well."

Cynthia was sort of in shock. She looked into Ava's eyes. They still had that pre-cry look...glossy, translucent, blurred with moist reflection. Cynthia almost said, "Wow," but then thought better of it. She felt like even the simplest verbal acknowledgement of Ava's melancholy would push her over the edge into tears. She wasn't against good cries in dark restaurants or bars...places that were a little less grandiose. Here it just felt too sad. The gleaming extravagance of the surroundings would shine a bright light on Ava's vulnerability and she didn't think Ava would want that.

Ava Dodd Radcliffe wasn't just looking for love, she was looking for a whole new *life*...new friends, new everything. Second Acts had never taken anything on of this scale. It

almost seemed like too much to ask...too much to hope for.
But Cynthia totally got it. She understood how Ava had
arrived at this juncture. Aside from Jonathon himself, a big
part of Ava's life had been dedicated to serving the Radcliffe
empire. Even the fun parts——the lavish entertaining,
celebrity-laden charity functions, the moving and shaking
with corporate and cultural elite——had all been Jonathon-
based, Jonathon-adjacent...all linked inextricably to the
Jonathon brand. When he died, a large part of Ava's world
must have just evaporated, or at least become painfully
irrelevant. She was walking around with a huge Jonathon-
shaped hole in her heart and in her life and she desperately
needed to fill it with something.

Cynthia loved a challenge, but this was a doozey. She
really wasn't completely sure it was a good idea. When it
came right down to it, she might not have said yes except
for one thing. She had an overwhelming desire to make Ava
happy. This was an integral part of who Cynthia was anyway,
but she had it bad for Ava. Even though they had never met,
in a way she felt close to her before she even walked into the
museum. Ava was the kind of celebrity you feel like you've
already spent time with. She had seemed knowable from the
very beginning of her career. She had the uncanny ability to

touch you right through a camera lens. And when Jonathon died, that quality only intensified. Some people shut down when tragedy strikes. They pull a curtain down and shut out the world. But Ava wore her grief prominently on her sleeve, on display for the entire world to see. There is no way to hide one's true self while subscribing to honesty under that kind of twenty-four hour, high-definition scrutiny.

Cynthia leaned forward, moving as close to Ava as the table allowed, and smiled a confident smile that said, *Yes, no problem, one new life coming up!* What she really said was, "Yes, of course...I'm in."

"Wonderful," replied Ava, closing her eyes for a moment in relief or appreciation. Then she reached over and lifted the silver lid off the cart Sutherland had parked nearby, revealing a spectacular display of pastries and cakes. "I think, by the way, that you should probably plan on being there, at least for the first one. I think a function like this needs a leader and if all goes as planned, I will be rather busy."

"Got it," said Cynthia. "I assumed I would be. I may bring my assistant as well."

"Perfect," said Ava, pushing a cream-colored, monogrammed, linen, business envelope across the table to

Cynthia. "A retainer to get us started." Then she indicated the cart with a slow, sweeping gesture, like a game show spokes-model. "Dessert?"

Chapter 7

Cynthia emerged from the shaded entryway of the museum and into the brilliant mid-afternoon California sun. She fumbled for her sunglasses in her purse. It was like stepping out of a matinee and being shocked that it was still daytime. She was a bit dizzy from the wine and the intoxicating nature of the assignment she had just accepted. She felt like she might be in over her head. Her method had always been to provide extremely personal service and she had a feeling that she was privy to the emotional lives of her clients far more than your typical matchmaker. But this crash course in Ava Dodd Radcliffe gave her pause. Although Ava was wonderful in many ways, Cynthia also thought it was possible that she might be a little unstable. Creating an entirely new social life, one that was decidedly more adventurous, might be just a new way of masking her sadness. It would constitute such a radical departure, Cynthia was afraid it might be risky emotionally for Ava while she was still clearly dealing with grief. Cynthia was very good at listening and nurturing and helping people find that special someone, but she was not a therapist. She had considered that as a career at one point and there were some similarities in the two professions, but she really didn't want to inadvertently cause Ava any more pain. She had to be very careful about who she brought into this plan. There would have to be a more rigorous screening process than ever before.

She had also felt a bit nervous that Second Acts was verging on becoming an escort service. She always thought there was a fine line that came with the territory, and this enterprise might test the limits. But how could she say no to Ava? She was basically weeping into her lunch, for god's sake. And when it came right down to it, Cynthia thought putting this whole thing together for her would be a lot of fun. Maybe too much fun. She did want to check in with an old friend who actually specialized in grief counseling...just to explain the situation and get his opinion.

She took the envelope out of her purse and opened it slowly. She peeked inside. It looked like one of those over-sized personal checks from massive leather checkbooks you see in movies from the forties, the size of an ancient photo album. The kind that Charles Foster Kane or Lionel Barrymore would use and then slam shut, like they'd just bought and paid for the entire world. The paper was thicker and lusher, like a wedding invitation, and the border decorations were more elaborately scrolled than normal checks.

She had absolutely no idea what to expect. They hadn't talked money at all.

She pulled it out and held it up.

$250,000.00

It took her breath away. Her hands trembled a bit. The only times she'd seen a check that big were in a real estate transactions and then the checks just fly across shiny tabletops and quickly vanish into escrow or someone's bank account other than one's own.

Ava's handwriting wasn't old fashioned. No old world flourish. It looked like she'd used a thin marker, not a quill or a fountain pen, and the letters and numbers were small and mousy, sort of too tight and precious for the grandiosity of the actual check and its monetary value. It reminded her of the work of shy arty girls from high school...more printing than cursive, controlled, precise, and perhaps revealing a fear of making mistakes or of being too flashy. Almost virginal. Well, that was obviously not the case with Ava Dodd Radcliffe, but she had married incredibly young and, although Cynthia hadn't delved too deeply into her past, she could totally see the sixteen-year-old Ava as a shy arty girl, quietly, sensitively driving all the crazy arty boys wild...from the introspective pimply ones, to the macho motorcycle-riding sculptors, and everyone in between, including a substantial percentage of the girls.

She wondered how she had even arrived at the figure. Was that her standard fee when embarking upon a long-term business relationship? Sort of monetary shock and awe. What did the chef get? The gardener? The captain of the Que Sera Sarong? The paperboy? She simultaneously felt lucky and like an underling in a way she hadn't with any of her other clients. Some of them were quite well off, but obviously nothing like this.

On the other hand, she did feel respected. A check for a quarter-of-a-million dollars is way better than a sharp stick in the eye. She was pretty sure anyway. Plus, if you stop and think about it, a billionaire writing a check for $250,000 is like spending $25 for a normal human.

As she pulled out of the parking space, she remembered she had turned off her phone for the meeting. She turned it on and descended the ramp. The phone rang as soon as it was finishing powering up.

It was her mother. Cynthia hadn't heard from her in a week and a half. Margie Amas had left Las Vegas, bound for Sicily, with her new fiancé——it still unsettled Cynthia to think of it——the notorious Hollywood hotel concierge and lothario, Dominic Orlando. He had wanted Margie to meet his family in his hometown. They were planning to tie the knot back in L.A. upon their return.

"Hi, Mom," she said, pulling up to the booth.

"I'm just calling to say hi," said her mother, or at least Cynthia was pretty sure that was what she said. The connection was not great.

"Eleven dollars," said the parking lot attendant.

"Hold on a second," said Cynthia, opening her purse.

"Hold on?!" screeched her mother. "We just started talking."

"No, Mom, wait..." She handed the attendant a fifty-dollar bill.

"I can't wait. I'm going out to dinner with Dominic and

his whole family and at least three of his old girlfriends. I'm going nuts over here!"

The attendant was counting out the change.

"That's sixteen, seventeen, eighteen, nineteen, twenty." He had obviously mistaken the fifty for a twenty. But he even shortchanged her for a twenty. The first bill he handed her was not a five, it was just another single. So he'd given her five dollars instead of the thirty-nine he owed her.

"Hey, wait, no, this isn't right."

"I know it isn't right!" screamed Margie. "Dominic has slept with half the town! Maybe still is! He has been disappearing for hours at a time..."

"Mom, hold on." She put the phone on the seat. "Listen, mister. I gave you a fifty. I know I did. I had one fifty in my wallet and now it's gone. But besides that, even if I had given you a twenty, you still stiffed me. You gave me five ones instead of a five and four ones."

"So now you're saying I owe you *five?*"

"No. You would owe me *four* if I'd given you a *twenty*. But I didn't, so you owe me *thirty-nine*. Well, thirty-*four* now. I think." Cynthia had consumed two glasses of wine and the small glass of Cointreau that Ava had brought out with dessert, and although her math was accurate, her skills of explanation were a bit impaired by the lubrication.

"CINDY! CINDY! DOMINIC WAS YOUR FRIEND! WHY DIDN'T YOU WARN ME ABOUT HIM!" She could hear her mother as clear as a bell all the way from Sicily, and the phone on the seat was not on speaker.

"Lady," snapped the attendant, "can't you at least choose a lie and stick with it?"

Cynthia had reached her limit. She held up her index finger, glared at the man, said, "Hold on, sir." and grabbed the phone.

"Mom! Are you insane? I mean more than usual? I *did* warn you about Dominic! Repeatedly! Passionately! I was totally against it! Good God! Well, at least you didn't marry him yet."

Stone-cold silence from Sicily. At first Cynthia thought the call had dropped out, but then she heard her mother breathing.

"Don't tell me you got married in Sicily! Mama mia!"

"I can't hear you, Cindy. Listen, I'm late for dinner. His mother is waiting for me. She's ninety-two. Even she warned me about Dominic. Why didn't you warn me? Whatever, I forgive you; besides, I do love him more than anything in the world. Okay, I gotta go...caio!"

Cynthia was beside herself. Her father had died when she was young and her mother's love life had pretty much died along with him. Margie had been alone and lonely ever since. She was desperately seeking someone, anyone, and had obviously been vulnerable to being swept away by the charming, but serially seducing Dominic.

"Jesus Christ!" said Cynthia, a little too loudly.

A short blast from a car horn...there were now two cars waiting behind her.

The parking attendant looked more worried now, like this angry, lying woman had suddenly transformed into a crazy, dangerous one.

He reached into the register and threw the fifty at Cynthia. The gate opened.

"Thanks," she said, counting out the dollars in her hand. "Okay, hold on, I need to give you some money now."

"No!" screamed the heavy-set attendant in a little-girl squeak. "Just leave. Leave now."

But Cynthia wanted to pay.

"No. I don't want special favors. I want to pay what I owe."

"Just get out of here!" said the attendant, now flushed with emotion.

Cynthia threw the money at him and pulled out. About two blocks down Wilshire she realized that she'd thrown back the fifty.

She didn't go back. Obviously.

Her phone rang. Lolita.

"Okay, Cynthia, spill the beans. Your meeting is over so why didn't you call me?"

"How in the world did you even know I was out?"

"Because you picked up! I've left you six messages. Come on: the 411 on Ava Dodd Radcliffe. I want it. I *need* it. I *crave* it. Give it to me. Now."

"Well..." said Cynthia. She proceeded to explain Ava's proposal. "To tell you the truth, I'm a little concerned about her. She has been through a lot. She wants me to put together social gatherings so she can meet people. The kind of people she doesn't usually meet. She put me on retainer. But I'm not positive that she's ready for this kind of thing. I wouldn't be."

"Well, *I* would," said Lolita without hesitation. "In fact, count me in."

"Oh, Lo, I'm not sure...everybody's supposed to be strangers to each other..."

Lolita snapped. "I *am* a stranger! I don't know Ava Dodd

Radcliffe! You are not going to keep me out of another one of these things!"

"When have I ever even done anything *like* this?"

"The whole Jack Stone thing. You kept me out of that. I'm the whole reason Stone came to you and you kept me out."

"But..."

"And I brought Ava Dodd Radcliffe in too."

"You what?"

"I just found out this morning from Tanya, that she mentioned you to her. Through her dog trainer, that is. But Tanya works for me. And she is spreading the gospel of Second Acts on my direction. In fact I've drilled it into her head." This was true. Lolita had been a huge promoter of Cynthia's business. She had sent many clients her way.

"Oh."

"So, like I said: count me in."

"Okay, okay," said Cynthia. "You're on the list."

Chapter 8

Lolita took a large gulp of coffee as she pulled up to international terminal six at LAX at 6:12 AM. She had been up since four. She tried to remember the last time she'd gotten up that early and then it came to her: never. She pulled into the airport parking structure.

She got to the revolving door where the passengers arrive, just down the way from baggage claim. She squinted up at the ancient arrival/departure screen. It was flickering and scrambled and almost completely unreadable. She looked around for an airline employee, but the only worker for as far as the eye could see was pushing a mop.

Lolita checked her phone for the flight info.

"Fucking Max," she said out loud. Of course she knew that it wasn't his fault that the flight had been delayed an hour and fifteen minutes. She was just pissed that she'd gotten up this early and now had to wait. The blaming Max part was more of joke, really. But what she hadn't noticed was that Max had texted her in the middle of the night saying that he had postponed his flight yet another *day*, due to an "unavoidable commitment." *Yeah, right, define unavoidable. Better yet, define commitment.* So, even though the hour and a quarter wasn't his fault, the twenty-four hours were. She would not have appreciated the irony that "Fucking Max" was currently fucking a twenty-nine-year-old Irish lass named Emily in a private dining room in the back of the historic Bleeding Horse Pub on Camden Street in Dublin. They were on the floor, bare naked and barely hidden by the two-hundred-year-old wooden table and chairs, a well worn oriental rug providing enough padding against the ancient stone floor, Guinness passed between tongues, its effects shared inside their heads, as he sang as much as he could remember of "The Wild Colonial Boy" before improvising additional verses intercut with outbursts of ecstasy. What had started as:

There was a wild colonial boy,

Jack Duggan was his name.
He was born and raised in Ireland,
In a place called Castlemaine.
Became:
There was a wild Californian boy,
Max Ramsey was his name.
Neither born nor raised in Ireland,
He'll fuck you just the same.

Emily was giggling with pleasure. She had told him when they'd met, leaning against the antique beer-soaked bar that, alas, no man had ever provided her with an orgasm. What she'd actually said with the most adorably forlorn expression you've ever seen, in the most charming and innocent brogue you've ever heard, was that "no fella has ever tickled my fancy in that special way, don't you know." Well, Max, of course, found this particular combination of undefiled beauty yearning to *be* defiled an unbelievably attractive nuisance. He could not let this challenge go unmet, even though he was already hell-bent on seducing her anyway, and even though he was almost sure she was lying. Later in his hotel room——under his teasing threat to deny her that which she claimed to never have had——she confessed that indeed she was. It had become pretty obvious when she screamed extremely specific instructions about little tweaks she'd prefer in his technique. And now here they were again back in the Bleeding Horse a week later later, this time circumstances demanding instant gratification, passions that could not, would not wait until they returned to the hotel, a mere block and a half away.

Back at LAX, Lolita sat down, slouching low in the hard plastic chair, and promptly fell asleep, her long legs stretched straight out in front of her. Only the rubber heels of her high black boots kept her from sliding onto the floor.

A little more than an hour later, the passengers on the flight from Dublin, the one that Max *would* have been on, deboarded. They passed through the revolving doors on the way to baggage claim, looking for loved ones. Seamus O'Brien was also looking around, but mostly scouting for movie stars, when he tripped over the outstretched legs of an American sleeping beauty. She woke up, helped him to his feet and they commenced to chat while she waited for Max.

"My friend should be coming along soon," she said. So Seamus waited with her. They hung around until every last passenger was accounted for and then Lolita took out her phone. She was going to call Max, but then finally saw the text.

"Fucking jerk," she said and then texted back:

OK. Maybe I'll be at LAX next time...maybe not.

"Man trouble?" asked Seamus with a smile.

"Is there any other kind?" replied Lolita.

She helped Seamus pick up Samuel Beckett from cargo. They discovered a common interest in dogs.

"Oh, God, I love Beagles," she said, kissing the dog on the lips.

"You seem to be in love with my dog," said Seamus.

"You have no idea," she smiled. "I like most dogs more than most people. I work with dogs. I was raised by dogs. I am not kidding." Lolita wasn't kidding. But she'd long stopped trying to explain to most people that Max the Irish wolfhound, King the Great Dane, and Wilfredo the Chihuahua were no ordinary canines. They had become her furry guardian angels after her father was imprisoned for perpetrating a Ponzi scheme upon his adoring and unsuspecting client base, (predating Bernie Madoff by decades) and her mother was institutionalized after her resulting nervous breakdown. Actually, guardian "angels" may not be completely accurate. Although the triumvirate do protect her and definitely have her best interests at heart, their inexplicable talents——ranging from miraculous to merely baffling——are sometimes useful, sometimes aggravating, but always at least partially problematic.

"Wow," said Seamus, "you win. I just, you know, *have* a dog. He's a good old dog. That's about it."

"Hey," said Lolita, wondering if she had rhapsodized a tad too much in the canine department, "I'm driving to Beverly Hills. Where are you headed?"

"To my brother's in a place called Los Feliz. O'Brien's. More like a pub than a café, apparently."

"Get out," said Lolita. "You're Donald's brother?"

"All my life. Is that close to Beverly Hills?"

"Oh, yes," she lied, "very close."

"Small world," he marveled as they walked briskly toward the parking garage. But the world was even smaller than he knew.

Chapter 9

TUESDAY LATE MORNING

The funnel-shaped lamps over the bar at O'Brien's Café on Franklin Street were vibrating and swaying. Patrons observed concentric circular waves in their coffee cups, suggesting the approach of *Jurassic Park* dinosaurs.

"Do you feel that?" asked one, looking up from his latte.

"This is the biggest one I've felt since I got here," said another.

A tourist dived under a table.

But this was no earthquake. The epicenter was directly overhead in the O'Brien apartment...more precisely at the intersection of Donald and Adriana, who were slamming each other with an enthusiasm and desperation consistent with a couple expecting a long-term out of town visitor any minute. On top of that, down the street Adriana's apartment was undergoing renovations.

"I...expect...we'll...be...doing...this...on...one... of...my... massage...tables...for...the...next...few... months," panted Adriana.

"I...would...do...this...on...a...train...and...I...would...do... this...in...the...rain," huffed and puffed Donald, "with... profound...apologies...to...Dr....Seuss."

Tommy, a recent hire at the café, also believed the rumbling to be a seismic geological event and was genuinely concerned, wondering about his boss's whereabouts, until he heard a howl in an unmistakable Irish brogue from upstairs, just as Lolita walked in with Seamus and Samuel Beckett.

Seamus looked up at the ceiling and said in his booming baritone, "It is truly a sound for sore ears that my big brother is having a good time here in these United States."

Lolita called her assistant Tanya to let her know that she would have to open the shop today. Then she and Seamus ordered breakfast, and Samuel Beckett curled up at her feet. It took one coffee's worth of conversation for Lolita to conclude that Seamus was gay. The tip-off was that he was showing no signs of being attracted to her and that almost never happened with Lolita.

"Lolita!" called Cynthia, walking in the door and getting in line at the coffee bar with Paloma, her new assistant. Paloma had grown up in inner city Los Angeles and then thrived at U.C.L.A. She was all brains, beauty, attitude, humor, talent...you name it.

Lolita rose to meet Cynthia and they hugged. "I thought you were meeting someone at the airport this morning," said Cynthia.

"Yeah, well, who needs him?" replied her friend. "I picked up this dashing bloke instead. Meet Seamus. He's a writer. He's come to conquer Hollywood. And this is Cynthia. And Paloma."

They shook hands all around. Seamus gave everyone his card, something he'd had done-up years earlier when he'd made a push in his writing career...a push that went nowhere.

"All the information on there is horribly defunct," he said. "Except for my name, my email address, and the fact that I'm a writer, if not by trade as yet, certainly by passion. Or delusion. Or both."

Cynthia tucked the card away and made a mental note: *A gorgeous, passionate writer from across the pond. A candidate for*

Project Radcliffe?

Seamus shook Paloma's hand quite a bit longer than he had Cynthia's. In fact, after they finished shaking they were still holding hands.

"Well," Paloma said to Seamus, "I'm an actress, so my entire life is dependent on fantasy. Maybe we can conquer Hollywood together."

"I have no doubt," he replied.

Lolita was suddenly quite sure that she had been wrong about Seamus' sexuality. She was instantly hurt that he had taken so quickly to the younger woman.

Sure, Paloma is beautiful, smart, and fifteen years younger. Maybe twenty. Who's counting?" I mean besides me? Probably him. But she doesn't have what I have. Whatever that is. I'll have to get back to me on that.

"Okay, Paloma," said Cynthia, hoping for a variety of reasons that what she was witnessing was not love at first sight, "we'd better get going. We have a lot of hearts to conquer today."

"Right, yes," she said, "but, Seamus, do come see me in this crazy musical I have the lead in."

"Jesus, Mary, and Johnny Cash," said Seamus, "don't tell me you sing too."

"She's an amazing singer," said Cynthia.

I can't sing thought Lolita.

"We're still work-shopping the play," shrugged Paloma. "It opens Friday after next. But you could come to the dress rehearsal this week. Or should I say *undress* rehearsal. It's sort of in the vein of *Hair* or *Oh, Calcutta*...lots of nudity. It's a musical comedy about the porn industry in the San Fernando Valley." She straightened into a comically old-fashioned theatrical pose as if preparing to project out into a large theater, and sang:

Go down in the valley,
The valley so low,
When they say 'Action!'
It's your turn to blow.

"Lyrics by Sondheim," she said.

Everyone laughed.

"Anyway," she said, "they haven't even decided on a title for the show yet. It'll either be *Going Down in the Valley*, *Porn Free*, or *Funny Money Shot*. What do you think?"

"I think I'm in love," said you know who.

Paloma was blushing noticeably as she and Cynthia departed.

Chapter 10

Two hours later and a half a block away, Cynthia sat at her new desk in her new office in the new headquarters of Second Acts Dating Services. She swung open the windows and breathed in the gorgeous world that lay before her. Such a view...not even a hint of the venal, cut throat underbelly of Hollywood. The downside was so well masked by the upside...the weather, the exotic greenery, and the sweet smell of orange blossom and success. Los Angeles was like that. Sometimes and in some corners it felt like Heaven on Earth and other times it unexpectedly veered off into what *Simpsons* creator Matt Groening called *Life in Hell*.

She knew that saying yes to Ava Dodd Radcliffe would

make an already heavy workload that much crazier. Paloma, who had only started a few weeks before, would need to really step up. Cynthia would have to give her a lot more responsibility or they'd be in trouble.

"Paloma, could you please come in here?"

She appeared around the corner in an instant.

"What's up, Boss?"

Paloma really was on it. Even though she was incredibly ambitious about her acting, she took her work at Second Acts very seriously too. She was smart, focused, and a wiz on the computer.

"Usually I'd tell an employee to please call me 'Cynthia'," said Cynthia. "But I kinda like it when you call me 'Boss'."

"Okay, Boss," laughed Paloma. "How do you feel about 'Boss Lady'?"

"Now you've gone too far. And by the way, I will call you 'Paloma', unless things get serious. Then I might call you 'Miss Rodriquez'?"

"No problem, Boss."

"Okay, so, Miss Rodriguez...about this Seamus fellow."

"The Irish bloke."

"Right," said Cynthia. "Well, I was thinking of asking him if he'd be interested in Operation Radcliffe. He's sort of the right type...cultured, handsome, charming. But I won't if you object."

"Object?" asked Paloma. "Why? I barely know the boy."

"Are you sure?" asked Cynthia. "Because I really don't want to screw anything up for you."

"Oh, no, I'm sure," said Paloma. "I'm not really looking for romance at the moment anyway." She did kind of like Seamus, but she already had a couple of hound dogs sniffing around her door and she was looking to simplify her life, not complicate it. Plus, she knew that Cynthia was a bit worried about the whole Radcliffe thing and wanted to be a team player for her.

"Okay, great then," replied Cynthia turning to her computer, clicking a few keys, and bringing up the roster for this week's dates. "Done. Let's get down to work. I need to get going on a proposal for Ms. Radcliffe. Providing her with "dates" would make a serious dent in the stable. I need to think about how to handle that. But meanwhile, you start arranging the regular dates for this weekend. As you know from watching me do this, every person's file is annotated with interests, favorite foods, musical tastes, hobbies, educational background...stuff like that. I've also added bullet points from their own interviews...highlights of their past romantic lives...things that went wrong, or right, or worst of all, signs of indifference. Disinterest or plain old boredom is much worse than downright dislike. Look at it this way: polar opposites repel, but if one of them flips, you've got serious attraction. On the other hand, two batteries that are dead to each other are just that, dead. You take a pass at it——I've done a lot of the upfront work and made recommendations for each——and then I'll review and tweak."

Paloma smiled. "I love you, Boss."

"Get to work, Miss Rodriguez. I need to get on the phone. Oh, I almost forgot. Would you be available to come along on this crazy adventure? I'll pay you double your hourly rate for the whole weekend. Not to participate, of course... just to assist me. We need to be there and also be available by phone for any of the normal clients on Saturday night. Most of them are scheduled for Friday, but there are a few. Anyway, the Radcliffe thing should be fun. I think."

"Oh, sure" said Paloma. "But the only thing is, my play opens the *following* Friday and we have a run-through this weekend, on Saturday morning, I have to check for the exact time. When and where?"

"Not sure where yet. Mid-afternoon probably. I think

you'll have plenty of time."

"It's a deal, Boss."

Chapter 11

Pete Blatt looked down from his balcony on the bustling afternoon Singapore traffic. The sea of humanity was making him seasick. He was tired of traveling. He and the band had played twenty-two major shows in fourteen countries in the past thirty days. And the tour had barely started.

He had gone out and bought a new phone and an iPad to enhance his video "chats" with Cynthia, but scheduling them had become more and more challenging. The time zone thing was hard to figure out anyway, and since Cynthia was busier than ever, when she did get a break, Pete was either asleep or on stage.

On top of that, being on a high-profile American rock tour is fraught with temptation. Women had been throwing themselves at him all day and night and his resolve was breaking down. Hotel pools and beaches were chock-full of bikini-clad maidens, usually more than three bed sheets to the wind. In some of the countries they'd been in, if you schedule a massage for lower back pain, chronic for Pete, the girl at your door *assumes* you want a happy ending. She's insulted if you turn her down. He fell asleep on the table once and woke up mid-orgasm, way beyond the point of even considering willpower. The other band members either had their wives and girlfriends with them or they were single and out for a wild time every night. There were only so many nights in a row of aborted video-chat sex that a red-blooded guitarist could take. After all, why did he pick up the guitar in the first place? Because piccolo players don't get laid, that's why.

Plus he wasn't taking care of himself. You know things are bad when the only vegetables you're consuming are one bite of the celery in your Bloody Mary at breakfast and the mint in your mojito at dinner. He had meant to run every morning and swim laps every night, but that had lasted exactly one day and no nights. His regimen had devolved into shuffling to the poolside bar and floating for hours on an inflatable raft like a sunbaked seal flopped on a rock.

This particular afternoon, he stumbled to the pool, but

even passing out onto a floatation device seemed far too ambitious. He collapsed onto a chaise instead——the new phone, clutched in his hand like a lifeline to home.

And it rang as soon as he dropped off, waking him...halfway waking him anyway. He peeled his face from the cushion and pried open one eye to peer into the screen. It was like he was searching a crystal ball for new hope from the future.

Cynthia Amas has requested a FaceTime session. Accept? Decline?

"Oh, accept, obviously," he said out loud, touching the screen, conjuring Cynthia's eager face a moment later.

Simultaneously, the young Thai woman on the chaise next to him——a possibly legal girl who had tracked him to the hotel after the concert the night before——thought he was talking to her. And since she had just asked him if he'd like her to apply sunblock to his back——a question he hadn't even heard, since he was sound asleep at the time——she squirted a large dollop of the white substance into her hand.

So, the image that materialized for Cynthia was this: a very young, very beautiful Thai woman rising from just beyond the sunburned, sweaty horizon of Pete's naked torso with a white viscous substance of questionable origin dripping from her slender fingers. To top it off, the girl was wearing a t-shirt proclaiming, "Guitar Players Make Me Hit the High Notes."

"Hi, baby," said Pete, in a voice like Tom Waits with laryngitis. "What's happening?"

At first, Cynthia was too stunned to answer, but when the Thai girl started rubbing the white substance into Pete's back, she was inspired to speak.

"This is what's happening," she said with cold finality. Pete's screen flickered, then went black.

He was in shock, or as much in shock as one can be while in a total state of exhaustion. He shook his head, trying to figure out what he'd said wrong, before drifting off to sleep again.

He woke up a few hours later and tried to call Cynthia back, but she didn't pick up. He too was struggling with the time zone issue. He thought he was fourteen hours ahead this particular day, but achieving certitude on the subject was challenging, especially since the time zone kept changing from city to city. At any rate, he didn't fully comprehend that it was two in the morning for Cynthia. She had turned off her phone an hour before and cried a little before falling asleep.

Chapter 12

WEDNESDAY MORNING

After watching about half of a very unfunny comedy, Max had fallen asleep and remained out for most of his transatlantic flight. His stopover at Kennedy was uneventful and then he slept even more of the five hours to Los Angeles. The only place he indulged in over-sleeping was on planes. Unless he happened to be seated next to a pretty woman... then he instantly turned on the full-press charm offensive.

For Lolita it was a replay of the other morning: god damn alarm clock that she only used on such horrible occasions, oversized travel mug of black coffee, and the mind-numbing half-asleep trek in stop-and-go (mostly stop) traffic from Beverly Hills. Except today she'd brought along her *dog*

Max, the Irish wolfhound. This way if the human Max weren't on the plane, at least she'd return with one Max from the Emerald Isle. But having one of her favorite canines along for company was the only thing good about it. Mornings like this were the exact reason she had nearly fled L.A., before solving the problem by starting her own business in a location that was within walking distance of her house. But she still resented going to the airport even if it was a once-in-a-blue-moon thing. It irritated her more than it should because, even though she knew intellectually that it was only temporary, she was an impatient woman. When she got stuck in traffic it literally felt to her that she would never get out of it, that she would be trapped forever, another miserable victim of Los Angeles...a small cog in the grand urban mechanism that ensures the miserable fate of those who live and die in L.A. in their stupid cars. If Max didn't show up this time she thought she just might lose her mind.

But this morning the flight came in early and Max was waiting for her, coincidentally sitting in the very same plastic chair that she had nearly slid out of and onto her legendary bottom twenty-five hours earlier.

He leaped up and ran to her. "My God, Lolita, my world

is complete again. I've missed you more than gloomy skies miss sunshine."

As corny and ridiculous as this exclamation was, it still charmed her. They threw their arms around each other and kissed, Max lifting her up and turning her around, her legs floating centrifugally, like a little kid.

"I feel like a military wife," said Lolita, "and that you've been deployed forever."

"I know," he said. "Well, I've been thinking of you every minute of every day I spent on the battlefield of commerce." He actually had thought of Lolita quite a lot, so it wasn't as big a lie as it would appear to anyone who knew the details of his sex life over the past weeks.

"I haven't looked at another man since you left," she also lied. She was less of a scoundrel than he was, but that was not saying much. First of all, she'd had a one-night stand with a customer who had come in with his Chocolate Lab just as the shop was closing the night after Max left. She'd turned off the lights, locked the door, and after popping a bottle of champagne from the fridge, they'd made love atop a large pile of fleece and foam doggie beds. A streetlamp and the red exit sign provided the only illumination, and it was even conceivable that she'd had her eyes closed for much of it, but *not looking at him at all* seemed unlikely. And second, if she'd had complete control over the puppet strings that ruled the actions of those around her, she would have been sleeping late in her bed with the younger O'Brien right now.

She and Max were made for each other in that sense. Both knew the other had no intention of being faithful, but they liked pretending they were. They were oddly comforted by each other's lies. Both somehow felt off the hook for their own.

As they kissed without the slightest concern for post-flight family reunions and general airport comings and goings all around them, Max, the dog that is, was on his hind legs, his front legs outstretched, with paws planted on Lolita's shoulders, looking a bit like he was trying to either dance with them or get deeper into the romantic equation.

"I don't think I can wait until we get to your place," said Max. "And traffic has got to be horrific still."

"Why, Max Ramsey, I do declare," cooed Lolita, getting all Scarlet O'Hara-ish, "I believe you are making untoward advances. What exactly are your intentions, kind sir?"

"My intentions shan't be uttered out loud in the presence of a southern belle of higher station such as yourself, ma'am. The etiquette here is to delay unsavory description until we are behind the closed doors of a local hotelier and your bloomers are properly ripped from your trembling flesh. In short, where is the freaking horse and buggy?"

They drove north out of the airport on Route One to Lincoln Avenue, looking for hotels. But the places near the airport, though perfectly acceptable for those on business trips or attending conventions, did not provide the proper ambiance that these two dedicated sensualists were seeking. So they forged on through Westchester, to Santa Monica.

"I've heard Shutters is nice," said Max, immediately realizing that, of course, Lolita was Cynthia's good friend. She might well know about Shutters' role in their relationship.

"Yeah," said Lolita, not at all angry or insulted, more like amazed, "I've heard it's a nice place to get a room with a girl, room number 14 perhaps, and keep it for fourteen days, only coming up for air for the occasional cocktail or to walk out a muscle cramp."

Max smiled, touching Lolita's shoulder...then face. "Hmm...I have no idea what you mean by that, darling," he said with faux dead seriousness. He knew her well enough to know that she wasn't mad. He also wondered if Cynthia would be jealous. And, if so, whether she'd be more jealous if they went to Shutters or someplace she'd never gone with him. Or not jealous at all. He didn't know so he just rolled a pair of imaginary dice. "Yes, well, anyway, there's a crazy rumor going around that Santa Monica has more than one hotel."

He lay down on his side on the car seat, placing his head face down in her lap. He spoke in the tone of a GPS system, conveying directions directly into her vagina.

"Proceed along Ocean Avenue, passing the absurdly over-rated Shutters on your left...I, for one, wouldn't think of patronizing the dump. *Bing-bing!* Continue, for several blocks, taking note of Palisades Park, overlooking the mighty Pacific Ocean. *Bing-bing!* The Camera Obscura, also on the left, then——*bing-bing!*——the lovely statue of Saint Monica herself, the namesake of the town. I think when she was very young, possibly under-age, she had a wild affair with Chaplin or somebody. Probably several somebodies."

Lolita couldn't believe that Max *the dog* was putting up with this. He would never have tolerated any other man being so intimate with her, especially in the close quarters of a car.

"Continue for three tenths of a mile," intoned GPS Max, "avoiding sun-dazed tourists, movie stars, and homeless jaywalkers and then——*bing-bing!*——take a right on

Wilshire Boulevard. Your destination, the Fairmount Miramar Hotel and Bungalows, is on your left. You have reached your destination. The route guidance has ended. *Bing-fucking-bing!*"

As Lolita pulled into the drive and got into a line of cars, Max nuzzled under her short skirt with his snout like a French pig searching for truffles. She started to push him away, but his warm breath felt good. There were four cars ahead of her and it seemed like only one valet on duty, so they had a few moments. She grabbed a pink and purple polka-dotted sweater from the back seat and placed it over his head, tucking it in around his head, pushing him down further for good measure, deep between her thighs.

He inhaled like he was ingesting a powerful drug and, for Max, that was pretty much what it was. He kissed her deeply, sloppily, slowly.

Three cars back.

Now his right hand came into play. Moving from knee to thigh. It was warm in there. He pushed his tongue against her, the moisture from inside and out quickly saturating the thin fabric. Max slid his other hand under her top, up her belly, under her bra, and over her breast...holding steady there, moving ever so slightly, then holding steady again.

The nerve endings of her flesh were perfectly in sync with his. With every tiny adjustment of his hands and mouth, she breathed in sharply, her lip trembling, her head tilting almost imperceptibly to one side, trying to contain her impulse to arch her back and slide deeper into the seat as the symphony of pleasure that he was orchestrating down below continued to build toward crescendo.

Two cars back.

"Max," she said, "you have to stop. We're getting close to the front. This is just a bit much."

But Max was merely the most persistent sexual instigator on the planet. He dove deeper, miraculously circumnavigating the damp cotton to pass through the right leg hole with his tongue...probing, searching in the warm, wet darkness. By the time he reached his destination, she was already ninety-nine percent there. So the rest, as they say, came easily. Fifteen seconds later, she let out a small sharp scream. One of her arms shot straight up, her fist hitting the car ceiling. Her right foot slammed down hard on the accelerator, causing a loud revving sound that startled the valet and patrons.

Max the dog let out a tiny yelp. Not threatening, not an expression of distress...more like he was duly taking note of Lolita's happiness. "Bing-bing!" said Max, kissing her a few more times, causing further spasms.

Luckily, she had put the car in park or they might have soon been on their way to the Santa Monica Police Station. Multiple charges of involuntary manslaughter are a damper to romance.

The valet approached. Lolita lifted Max's head off of her lap, sweater and all. He looked like he was wearing a brightly colored, absurdly unorthodox burqa. Lolita's face was flushed. Afterglow was written all over it.

"Hello, Madame, are you checking in?"

"No, I mean yes. Obviously yes."

Max pulled the stifling garment from his sweaty face. His hair was hilariously askew. He looked like a cat crawling in out of the rain.

"I guess that's why they call it a sweater," he said.

"Oh, hello, David. Is bungalow seven available?"

Lolita rolled her eyes. Max was apparently a regular everywhere in Santa Monica. Probably everywhere on Earth.

"Oh," said the valet, obviously surprised to see an old friend. "Mr. Ramsey, good to see you again. Yes, I believe seven is available. But if not, I'm sure we can find something else to your liking."

Lolita and Max got out of the car. Lolita tried to flatten her skirt, using her hands like two ineffective irons. Max the dog followed along behind...no leash, but totally well behaved, like he was just another member of the entourage.

"David, this is Lolita. Like the book...only better. I just read one of her best chapters."

"Very nice to meet you," said David. "Welcome to the Miramar. How long will you be with us?"

"Who knows?" asked Max, shaking David's hand as he and Lolita headed for the entrance. "Three hours, three weeks, three years? Life is a mystery. Love is ten times that. Garbo lived here for *four* years...should we try to break that record?"

Lolita shook her head and rolled her eyes as they crossed the lobby. But she also smiled. "We have to get out of here by Saturday morning at the latest. I have a party on a yacht to go to."

"Whose yacht?" asked Max, stopping dead in his tracks.

"Nobody special," she teased.

"Oh, come *on*," he said. "What's the difference? You know I'll get it out of you eventually. Come *on*."

He was right. They were a terrible combination when it came to keeping secrets. His prosecutorial passion to find things out dovetailed perfectly with her desire to reveal. Whenever Lolita held something in, she felt she might literally burst apart. And he was like a prisoner digging away at the wall of his cell with a nail file. He would chip and chip until a tiny crack revealed the smallest ray of sunshine. And then he'd dig harder, with more intensity, until the entire wall came down, chances are revealing more secrets that you were even trying to protect in the first place.

"Come *on*, Lolita. Don't I share everything with you?"

This was so patently absurd that they both burst into laughter.

"But really, Lolita, you know you want to tell me. Come on. I'm not going to let up for one second until you do. In fact, I will not leave this lobby."

He sat down in the middle of the floor. "Come on. Come on. Come *on!*" Max the dog sat down next to him.

Patrons were forced to walk around them.

"For god's sake," said a young woman pushing an elderly woman in a wheel chair, having to negotiate between man, dog, and a couch.

"Don't blame me," said Max, rolling his eyes and tipping his head toward Lolita, "it's all her fault. She tripped me and my guide dog here. I'm considering pressing charges."

"Okay, okay," she whispered, a bit embarrassed, but also trying not to laugh out loud. She slapped him on the side of the head, not hard enough to hurt, but not really that softly either. "You have to promise me you won't tell anyone."

"I promise," he said standing up.

"And I cannot bring you along. This is totally an invite-only thing. No guests allowed. Period."

"All right! Who cares? I don't even *want* to go. I'm not a big boat fan."

"Oh, really?" said Lolita in a low voice. "Well...it's only the yacht of one Ava Dodd Radcliffe."

This actually stunned Max, someone who is almost impossible to stun.

"Wait. This is epic. How did you happen to be invited?"

"Never mind."

"Come on. Do you want me to sit down again? I'll *lie* down this time."

"Okay, but you can't tell her I told you."

"Tell who?" Max's eyes got wide. "Oh...so this is a Cynthia Amas production?"

Lolita didn't say anything. She just walked toward the check-in desk, Max the dog at her heels. Max the man caught up to them and kissed Lolita's neck.

"Good afternoon, Mr. Ramsey," said the young woman behind the desk. "Did you enjoy your swim?"

Max and Lolita gave each other perplexed looks, but then realized how sweaty and drippy Max was and understood the confusion.

"Yes, Megan," said Max, putting his arm around Lolita's waste. "I was practicing my diving."

"We might have to schedule another session," said Lolita, slapping and shooing Max's hand away from her backside, when she realized he was slowly moving it southward, sneaking his fingers under the hem of her skirt. "He's got a lot to learn."

"Oh, I'm sure he does," said the girl with a smile. This was the kind of familiarity that would be unthinkable with any other guest. Max was a special case. She registered them without asking another question. "Bungalow seven it is. Here are two keys. Check out time is...well...whenever you want it to be I guess. Will your dog be needing any special foods or accommodations?"

"No," said Lolita, "room service will be fine. He eats human food."

Max interjected: "He eats better food than 99% of the world's humans."

"Got it," said the girl.

As they walked out of the lobby, Max's phone rang. He looked down at it. "Ugh...Emily," he said, sending it to voicemail.

"I'll bite," said Lolita. "Who's Emily?"

"She's just some girl."

"Wait, I thought Emily was the dog on the phone in Dublin."

Max was momentarily confused. "Oh, right the hotel dog. Yes, that was Emily too. But Emily was also an assistant in the office. She keeps calling...bothering me with stupid details that I don't need to know about. I don't know what her problem is."

Lolita rolled her eyes. "I have a feeling her problem is you. Just a guess. You're almost everybody's problem."

"Me?" asked Max, pretending to be hurt. "Don't be silly. I'm almost everybody's *solution*." He put his arm around her, kissed her, and reached down to scratch behind the dog's ear as they crossed the garden to bungalow number seven.

Chapter 13

WEDNESDAY LUNCHTIME

Cynthia stared at her computer screen while picking at the salad that Paloma had delivered from down the block. The neighborhood was a good one for variety. It would take months to get into a rut.

There were more than seven hundred names in the Second Acts database. That number was fluid, because people kept signing up, while others paired off, and those would not be taken off the rolls until their membership expired.

For Operation Radcliffe, Cynthia would cross-reference the records for artistic, literary, cultured types who also happened to be sexually adventurous. She had a thought.

She wrote an email:

Hi Ava:

Putting together your first event. I think we may have covered this, but just to make sure. If two individuals meet at one of your soirees, I don't think you or I should stand in the way of them making subsequent one-on-one dates together. Make sense?

Cynthia

Then she went back to selecting names that fit the guidelines she had set. Unfortunately, there were at least two clients involved in this weekend's dates who would have fit in nicely at a Radcliffe affair:

Ingvild Hamsun, a Norwegian visual artist and intellectual, had signed up about a month ago. She was a visiting professor at U.C.L.A. and had come from a wild background that included years in a free-love commune in Sweden immediately following her college years. She had listed her sexual preferences as "varied."

If her date with Tony Barlow, a mystery writer and fiction teacher at Occidental, went nowhere, she would ask Ingvild if next time she'd like to be involved. She scrolled through Tony's biography.

Longshoreman, bus driver, Harvard graduate, Iraq war protestor, itinerate boxer, newspaperman, travel writer, mystery writer...this guy is open to anything. Maybe he is on the right wavelength for the Ava adventure too. But I can't exactly pull that on them after their date together has been confirmed:

"Hi, sorry about this, but you know how I put you two together through my patented ultra-personal method of matchmaking because in my estimation you have the makings of a long-term love connection? Yeah, well how would you feel about cancelling that date together and being potential pawns in the fantasy of an obscenely rich and possibly unhinged woman instead?

She could not, would not ask them that question.

Then she remembered that there were several clients, maybe more than several, who had so far been difficult to match. Men and women whose pasts and predilections were less compatible with others...somewhat worse bets for monogamy. Every time one of their names popped up as a possible match for someone, there was something about them that wasn't quite right. And it just occurred to Cynthia that the unifying factor of these people was that she doubted their sincerity about wanting to find a long-lasting, more or less permanent relationship. And, of course, because that was what she had been looking for, she'd passed them by, thinking that next time, with the right partner, they might be more *right*.

Well, maybe this is next time. Maybe these birds of a feather would flock well together. Since people often fall in love when they're not looking to, maybe a group of "not-necessarily-lookings" would result in surprisingly strong pairs. She loved how counterintuitive, yet thoroughly feasible the logic behind this was.

She had flagged those clients as "complicated."

Searching "complicated."

Searching…searching…

Bingo: two hundred and eleven "complicateds."

She smiled.

I believe Operation Radcliffe is underway.

Plink. Email from Ava.

That was quick.

Cynthia-

Oh, absolutely. That was the whole idea. Let the love chips fall where they may. As you know, I am not strictly interested in finding a special someone anytime soon——but I'd be delighted to see it happen to others. It would renew the group with fresh faces for next time, for one thing. Also, it occurred to me that the first soiree could happen on one of my yachts, Que Sera Sarong. Sorry about the dumb name. My husband named it, so I blame him. I must confess I like it, though. Anyway, it's docked in Long Beach, so we could head out into the open sea a bit, then north along the coast, and then back down. Short and sweet, but still a fun outing. Sutherland will be on board with his team. It sleeps thirty, plus captain and crew.

Cheers,

Ava

Wow. Her yacht sleeps thirty. Excuse me: one of her yachts. I wonder how many the entire fleet sleeps.

Plink. Another email.

Ava is becoming a real chatterbox.

Cynthia-

Also, I just found out that I'll be leaving the country for a few weeks. I'm leaving next Wednesday. So if the Que Sera Sarong thing could happen this weekend, maybe a Saturday-Sunday cruise, that would be fantastic. I know it's short notice, but I have complete confidence that you can pull it off. Let me know if there's anything I can do to help with the preparations. I'll alert Sutherland and the crew. And I'll forward their contact information. Also, the LACMA show opens on Friday. I'd be honored if you would come.

Thanks again.

Can't wait.

Ava Dodd Radcliffe

My God. This weekend? Impossible. Totally impossible. I would have to be stark raving mad to agree to that.

Cynthia quickly composed a reply.

Dear Ava-

Okay, great, no problem. This weekend it is.

Cynthia

Okay. Friday: the erotic art opening, and the normal weekly dates that same night. Saturday: more weekly dates and then some kind of floating mixer-odyssey for thirty.

Monday: check myself into a loony bin. Straightjacket, optional.

Cynthia was in a bit of a daze when Paloma came around the corner.

"Hey, Boss, are you all right?"

"Oh, yeah, just lost in thought."

"Okay, well, Lolita's on line two. By the way, I've got preliminary itineraries for Friday's dates. They're in "dates in progress." There really wasn't much to do...you left extensive notes. You didn't tell me you'd already basically worked it all out, Boss. But when you get a chance, give them a look and if you're good with it, I'll start making reservations."

"Awesome, Paloma," she said as she punched line one. "Hello, Lo. What's up? Did Max finally straggle in?"

"Oh, he did a lot more than straggle, sweetie," replied Lolita. "In fact, I'm with him right now."

"You took him home?"

"No, actually we're at the Miramar..."

"Oh. That's nice. Give him my regards."

"But I'm calling about something else. My *dog* Max, the wolfhound, disappeared. Max——the man I mean——and I were, you know, fooling around for, you know, a while. And Max the dog was asleep on the couch. He was with us and then suddenly wasn't. With us."

"Well, your dogs are known for that, aren't they? He probably made his way to your house. Or your shop."

"Yeah, I just got off the phone with Tanya. He's not at the shop, but she's heading over to the house."

"Well, I'm sure he..."

"Hold on, Cynthia...she's calling."

Beep.

Cynthia turned back to her computer screen and opened dates in progress. It looked pretty good. Paloma was right; Cynthia had forgotten that she'd done most of it already. But she rechecked and made a few more adjustments, Cynthia switched around a restaurant here, a club there, and cultural events, here, there, and everywhere. She utilized a blend of data and intuition that could not be taught.

Beep. Lolita was back and now she was distraught.

"Cynthia! All three dogs are gone!"

Chapter 14

Donald O'Brien's café was uncharacteristically empty, but he was fine with that. He and Adriana were catching up with Seamus.

"So, how much do you know about this Paloma girl?" asked Seamus, taking a large sip of Jameson, and then chasing it with black coffee.

"I know I like her," said Adriana.

"I know *I* like her," said Donald a bit too enthusiastically

Adriana raised an eyebrow.

"Oh, for Christ's sake, I like her for my little brother," he said.

"Well," said Seamus, "she asked me to come see her in her

dress rehearsal tonight. Is that too creepy? Going to see her in a play about porn and then asking her out? This question is directed at Adriana, Donald. We already know you're too creepy."

"Very funny," said Donald.

Adriana laughed. "Maybe you should ask her *before* you see it."

"Good point," said Donald. "Plus, after the play there'll probably be a line a mile long of horny theater geeks wanting to beat you to it. And by 'it' I mean…"

"Okay, Donald…another good point," murmured Seamus, staring past his brother and his girl at nothing.

But then all of a sudden, *something* was in his line of vision. Well, three things: an Irish wolfhound, a Great Dane, and a Chihuahua wearing a bowtie.

The three dogs were sitting at attention, as if they'd been there for a while, staring straight at Seamus, growling softly, locked in eye contact. They occupied a spot on the café floor that was positively canine-free moments before. They knew that Lolita had a thing for Seamus and they were not at all happy about it. They liked Max…the man that is. He was really the first man in Lolita's life who they all agreed on. This was their preemptive way of scaring Seamus out of the running with her. They had no idea that he was clueless as to what point their appearance there was supposed to be making. Nor that he wasn't even interested in Lolita to begin with.

"Bloody hell," said Seamus, pointing with a trembling finger. "Where the fuck did they come from?"

Donald and Adriana turned around.

"Who?" they asked together.

Seamus gasped. The dogs were gone.

He got up from his bar stool and moved toward the spot to get a closer look. As if being closer would change anything.

"Jesus, Mary, and Casper the Friendly Ghost," he murmured.

"Donald," whispered Adriana out the side of her mouth, "what's little brother babbling about?"

"Damned if I know," he replied. "He does have an artistic temperament."

Seamus turned around. He'd already made the decision not to try to describe the vision he'd just beheld.

"You know what? I'm tired," he said, returning to the bar. He poured himself a bit more Jameson's. "I've had a long day. It's four in the mornin' to me."

"Yeah, you're right," said the older brother. "Why don't

you hit the hay? I mean the couch. We'll be up in a bit."

"I believe I'll take you up on that," said Seamus, grabbing his suitcase from the corner and waking up Samuel Beckett who had been asleep behind the bar for hours. "The more I think about it, there's no way on Earth I'll make it to that play tonight. Too bushed. I'll have to see it after it opens."

"But there's nudity, for Christ's sake," said Donald, incredulous. "I'm sorry, Adriana, but come on."

"Nah," said Seamus, "I'm zonked. I'll come back for the dog kennel later."

"Don't bother," said Donald. "I'll stick it in the back room down here. There's not a whip of storage upstairs."

"Good night, all," said Seamus hugging them both and stepping out onto the busy Franklin Avenue sidewalk. He turned left, heading toward the side door entrance to the upstairs apartment and crashed into a pedestrian.

It was Paloma.

"Jesus, I'm sorry," said Seamus, amazed to see her again so soon.

"You can call me Paloma," she smiled.

"Well," he said, crossing himself and dipping slightly in a partial genuflection, "meeting you was a religious experience."

"Right," she replied. "So this is the famous blarney I've heard so much about."

"If only I had a stack of bibles on me," he said, "I'd prove you wrong."

"Yeah, well, I've gotta get going. I'm on my way to the theater. Are you coming tonight?"

Her beauty hypnotized Seamus. He instantly changed his mind. How could he have even *considered* not going?

"I wouldn't miss it for the world. Two things, though. One...when and where the hell is it? And two...what and where are we going afterwards?"

"You do not waste any time," she said, smiling and thinking about how Cynthia would be disappointed if Seamus weren't involved in Operation Radcliffe.

"Life is short," he said. "Plus, I wager after tonight, every Tom, Dick, and lots of *other* Dicks will be knocking on your stage door."

Paloma blushed and looked down at her feet.

Seamus wondered if he'd gotten too vulgar with that last dumb quip. Donald's influence, he thought.

"Umm . . ." he said, touching her shoulder, "sorry about that."

But she looked up, touched one of his cheeks with her

hand and kissed the other. She pulled a piece of scrap paper out of her wallet and wrote down the address of the theater. "Eight o'clock curtain. I'll put you on the list. See you after the show," she said, heading toward her car.

Seamus smiled. He felt welcomed in this new world. Los Angeles had such a horrible reputation in Ireland. Telling people you were moving there was tantamount to saying you were relocating to Hell, or at least Purgatory. But so far he'd found it to be delightful. He watched her disappear around the corner and then looked down at the card.

The Hollywood Theater

Make Hay Productions

1146 North McAdden Place

Hollywood, California

He would go upstairs, throw some water in his face, grab a quick snack, and head out. As he turned toward the building's entrance, he looked back down at the scrap of paper, turning it over in his hand.

The word "Jack" was written on it five times and each "Jack" had a heart drawn around it. He closed his eyes and shook his head. "Who the hell is Jack? Jesus, Mary, and fuck my life," he said out loud as he climbed the stairs.

Chapter 15

"King! Max! Wilfredo! Come!" yelled and screamed Lolita and Max from the pink Vespa they had shared once before under much happier circumstances. They crisscrossed Beverly Hills——up Canon, across Carmelita, down Roxbury, over to Rodeo via Brighton Way, then past her dog grooming shop, and on and on around the neighborhood. This time Max was driving, so that Lolita could keep a closer look out for her babies. "King!! Come here!! Max! Wilfredooooo!"

"Oh, Max," she sighed, pressing her forehead against his back, "if I don't find them, I swear, I can't go on."

"Don't worry, baby," he said over his shoulder, in a tender tone that Lolita was truly touched by, "we'll find them. I promise." He sounded all the world like a normal, concerned, dedicated boyfriend.

She hugged him harder around his waist.

He was shocked by how much he liked it.

Chapter 16

Seamus got to the tiny theater a little bit late. As he approached the box office, he reached for his wallet, only to find that the four hundred-odd American dollars that had been in there had vanished.

"What the bloody hell?" he said.

"Excuse me?" asked the seriously pierced-face ticket seller, who had been deeply engrossed in a biography of Antonin Artaud. "What did you just say to me?"

"No," said Seamus. "I wasn't talking to you. My money seems to have evaporated. I must have left it back at the place." He reached around in his pockets, pulling out a few mangled bills. "How much is it?"

"It's free," said the gloomy Artaud lover. "This is just a dress rehearsal. But you have to be on the list."

"Oh," said Seamus. "Right, I knew that. Okay, well I'm Seamus O'Connor."

The kid scanned down a list on a yellow legal pad. "Nope, sorry."

Even upside down, Seamus could see his name as plain as day.

"That's me, right there," he said, reaching through the window and pointing to his name.

"Oh, okay, whatever," said the kid. "Halle-fucking-lujah."

Unfortunately, the play had already started and the usher wouldn't let him enter until intermission. But Seamus persisted. The guy got the house manager and she was also adamant about enforcing the rule, until Seamus poured on the charm. She was a sucker for the brogue anyway, but then she found out he had a dog named for her favorite playwright. And then Seamus started actually *quoting* Beckett. First, a play on one of his titles: Instead of "I Can't Go On, I'll Go On," he said, "I Can't Go In, I'll Go In," which immediately made her laugh. Then, "There is something...more important in life than punctuality, and that is decorum." The title and quote were so ridiculously appropriate for the occasion, she immediately dug a flashlight out of the box office drawer and escorted him to the middle of the front row.

There were young men made up to look middle-aged on stage holding movie cameras, just finishing a musical number that ended with the line...

"And that's why we love sex!"

...at the top of their lungs, with every bit as much Broadway bravura as one would expect from, "No, no, no, *no way* I'm livin' without you!" or "Hooray for Hollywood!"

The stage went black and the thirty-odd people in the audience clapped enthusiastically. A pin spotlight popped on, illuminating the tiniest patch of flesh dead center stage, about five feet away from Seamus. A naked body was moving in slow motion, the spot traveling with it, showing off new body parts, slowly, seductively, like a striptease in which darkness is removed instead of clothing. At first he wasn't even sure if this were female flesh, but then——oh, yes, bingo——it was. The next little mystery was whether or not this was Paloma. He, of course, hoped it was.

And it was.

The spot widened to reveal her and she launched into a ballad relating the young porn star's backstory:

I knew when I was very young,
That acting was my game,
I learned my lines and hit my mark,
From Tulsa to Tulane.

As she continued, Paloma walked down a small staircase and stopped right in front of Seamus.

I traveled west to L.A. town,
Real life is so complex,
I finally got my Shakespeare down,
But all they want is sex.

Sure, the lyrics were silly. In fact, Seamus completely missed the next verse. He was enchanted. And not because a beautiful coffee-brown naked woman was dancing so close he could count the goose bumps on her nipples. Or because she had a lovely voice and tremendous poise and presence. Or because the song seemed to be based on an Irish or Scottish folk melody that he could not quite put his finger on. Or even because he thought he might be falling in love with her. No, this was it: he wanted to write something for her. He could see her becoming a star.

She moved to the other side and climbed another set of stairs, heading for center stage again.

So ring around the casting couch,
And ready on the set,
I swear that there will come a day,
I haven't seen as yet.

That when my agent calls me,
To inform me of my luck,
The role that I have landed won't,
Require a flying fuck!

As she sang that last line, she took two quick steps, and leaped, doing a cartwheel, a handspring, and a flip. Just then, a spotlight illuminated an actor, lying on his back on a high platform bed, and Paloma landed, straddling him in the classic woman-on-top position, her hands high in V-for victory position, both of them screaming, "YES!" in unison, to thunderous applause. Well, as thunderous as thirty people can get.

The only person in the audience not clapping was Seamus. He was dumbstruck. Aside from the fact that he was immediately jealous of the actor beneath her at the moment, he could not believe his good fortune. Paloma was beautiful, smart, talented, and a goddamn *gymnast*, for god's sake. "God bless the United States of America," he said out loud, causing the applause to swell again.

Chapter 17

Cynthia had worked long into the night planning Operation Radcliffe. She had already contacted Will Grover, her set decorator friend. He had agreed to add a few touches to the yacht to convey a bit of mood and ambience, even though Cynthia had the feeling it had plenty of that in its natural state. She had connected Will with the ship's captain and they were meeting on the dock in Long Beach first thing in the morning. She had composed an email to all the possible participants and then personalized it for each of them. For instance:

Hi Antonio-

I hope this finds you well. I have been carefully developing a list of possible dates for you and will get it to you next week.

But I am writing about something else.

I am putting together an event for a wealthy client. This will be a two-day party (short notice, this Saturday and Sunday) and will take place mostly upon a luxury yacht. Participants will drink, dine, and socialize with the hostess and at least eleven other attractive, intelligent, fascinating men and women. Good conversation and much, much more.

She has authorized me to invite anyone who I believe would be a good fit and I believe you would. There are twice as many invitees as spaces, so, if you are interested,
RSVP ASAP. OK?
Best,
Cynthia
P.S. If you at all are prone to seasickness, you should probably respectfully decline or BYOD (bring your own Dramamine).

She sent twenty-five emails in all, including to Seamus, and then looked at the time. It was late. Time for bed. She would get up early to check for responses.

But then her phone rang.

"Hello, Mom. How's it going over there?"

"You won't believe what happened, Cindy."

"Oh, I think I would."

"Dominic and I were eating dinner with his mother and a couple of his siblings and some cousins...a very large group. There were some other women there who came in together... they ranged from early twenties to older than me. Five in all."

"Let me guess, ex-girlfriends?"

"Well, yes. But that wasn't the surprising thing. The conversation went from topic to topic...at first just a lot of bragging about Sicily...the history, like the Greek period, the Byzantine period...up until the unification with Italy. It really is fascinating. Dominic was translating for everyone."

"Mom, it's like four in the morning here. I really need to get some sleep."

"I know, Cindy, I know, but then his mother started talking about what he was like when he was a kid. And then one of the women, a big fat huge one, said that she was in the same grade as he was. And that she was his girlfriend when he was a teenager. And then somehow it came out that she had gotten pregnant."

"Oh, God."

"And then another one said the same thing."

"Oh, God again."

"He had gotten four of those five women pregnant. The fifth one was one of his children. And *she* has a child. His *grandchild!*"

"Oh, Mom. Look. Calm down. Get on a plane and come back here by yourself!"

"I can't, Cindy! We're leaving in two days for Venice!"

"What?!" Cynthia was now lying on her back on the couch, holding the phone with one hand and covering her face with the other.

"I've never seen Venice!" shrieked her mother.

"Mom!"

"Cindy, I've already decided!"

"Well then why did you even *call* me?!" Cynthia couldn't take much more of this.

"We're going to Venice and then we'll see about the rest."

"Mom, what's there to *see* about? You are married to a serial liar and philanderer! We now know more than we did before, but I've always known he was a bad bet for marriage!"

"Well, if you *knew* that, why didn't you *tell* me?!"

Cynthia was afraid her head might explode. She sat straight

up again.

"Mom, all I can recommend is that you get on a plane by yourself and come home. You can stay with me if you want. Get the hell away from Dominic Orlando!"

"But Dominic didn't even *know* about all these pregnancies. He was as shocked as I was. He's not even sure the seven kids are all his!"

"Seven?"

"Yes, but a couple of them don't even look like him. There's definitely some hanky-panky going on around here."

"Oh, you think? Mom, come home. Please. Come. Home."

"Why do you want to keep me from seeing Venice?"

"Mom."

"Okay, okay. But one more thing. I've been thinking about it. I actually *want* a grandchild. And I don't see me getting one out of you. So..."

"What?"

"Don't you want a little sister?"

"Mom, she wouldn't be my sister! Do I even have to explain that to you?"

"Okay, now you're making fun of me."

"Mom, no. I just need to go to bed. I'll call you back."

Cynthia hung up and fell onto her back on the couch again. She was incredibly tired. It almost felt like she had dreamt the entire conversation.

She imagined entire boatloads of Orlando kids and grandkids crossing the Atlantic in a giant fleet. They all looked exactly like their father or grandfather, little carbon copies of Dominic, and they were all calling her "Big Sister Cynthia," in strong Sicilian accents. Somewhere in there she had, of course, fallen asleep.

Chapter 18

The light streamed in through a whole different hotel window, casting a shadow of palm fronds and Venetian blind slats on the opposite wall.

Seamus opened one eye to the miniature mountain-landscape-like view of tousled off-white sheets, comforter, and the loveliest ass he had ever seen. The post-show dinner and drinks with Paloma had gone well. Very well. He could not bring himself to invite himself to her place and was not about to offer half of his brother's couch to her, so they ended up in a nearby hotel, the Sunset Marquis.

He reached over and placed his palm upon one of Paloma's perfect cheeks, cupping it in silent reverence and admiration...remembering the night before. How deeply moved he'd been. And she had been too, he thought. This bottom was far greater than any work of art he'd ever seen, read, or listened to. He moved his hand slowly to the small of her back, studying that perfect slope, housed in perfect skin, altered only by a tiny tattoo of a bluebird in flight. He hadn't seen it the night before as they'd rocked in the 2:00 AM silence and now it was like a visual representation of the luck that had been bestowed upon him since the moment he'd touched down in this supposedly hard and uncaring town.

Good luck in Hollywood is the luckiest luck there is. The softly singing birds outside helped complete the sensation. He had no idea what kind of birds they were, but he decided they were blue.

He moved closer and kissed her shoulder softly, causing two fingers on her right hand to react slightly, as if a tiny electrical pulse had animated them.

"Hey, lover man," she mumbled, her face still smooshed deep into the mattress.

Seamus reached for his phone.

"Hey," he said. "Want to get some room service?"

"No, no. You don't want to spend any more money...you're a starving artist just like me."

"Yes, well," he said, kissing her neck, just behind her ear, "don't worry about it. I've got it covered."

"My Irish sugar daddy, huh?" Then she jerked her head upward. "Hey, what time is it?!"

"Oh," he whispered, "I imagine it's ten or ten-thirty."

"On Friday?!" she squealed, rolling off the bed and running to the bathroom, "Jesus, I'm late for work! I've gotta go!"

"Can't you just call in sick?"

"No! Cynthia is depending on me." She jumped into the shower, instantly covering herself with soapsuds and rinsing them even faster. By the time Seamus got there, she was out and drying off.

He insisted he'd help out, grabbing a second towel and wrapping her like the warm delicacy she was. He managed to stop her for one long second to kiss her passionately on the lips, and despite her panic, she paused to enjoy it.

She looked down and smiled.

"Mr. McFun doesn't know I'm late for work.

"He's got a one-track mind, I'm afraid," Seamus replied, letting the towel drop to the floor.

"I tell you what," she said, kissing his chest, sliding her hand down his firm abdomen to his even firmer Mr. McFun, "how about a quickie?"

"'Quickie'" is not in Mr. McFun's lexicon," he smiled, leaning down, kissing her breast and caressing her waist so sweetly, so perfectly, that Paloma breathed in deeply through her nose and then sighed out, trembling... instantly persuaded to surrender a good deal more lateness to him. Although they'd just met, she was deeply struck by his devotion to satiate her carnal hunger. No one had touched her this way. Ever.

They moved back toward the bed, but never made it that far, winding up on the carpet...she, facedown, his warm breath on her legs, his lips finding the bluebird. He concentrated on that spot for some time, regretting that he'd missed it the night before. Theirs was the kind of brand-new desire that requires almost no foreplay. The bluebird's happiness seemed to spread...every inch of them instantly alert, completely in play, hard, soft, warm, wet, anticipating, reacting, alive. As he gently turned her over, moving up and making initial contact, he hesitated, holding back, massaging the beginning of her with the end of him, all parts yearning for total engagement, but waiting for an eternal five seconds before mutually driving everything all the way home.

She cried out. Seamus slowed down again, lifting his head from where it had burrowed deep into her neck to look at Paloma. He loved the face of a beautiful woman at the moment of climax, but he had never seen anything quite like the vision before him now. Her features distorted almost beyond recognition with pleasure...but still breathtakingly beautiful: eyes squeezed tightly, nose crinkled, cheeks flushed, teeth pinning lower lip in place. He pushed up higher inside her, then higher still, wanting to watch her respond, her face morphing into still more exquisite variations on itself. He felt happier at that moment than maybe he'd ever felt...dizzy, euphoric, and privileged to be bearing witness.

"Seamus!" she cried. "Would you mind wrapping this up?! I'm late!"

And Seamus did wrap it up, letting everything go, he reached out to grab onto the back of the couch and thrusting harder than ever, their cries were as intertwined as their body parts.

Before they knew it they were on their backs, staring at the ceiling. He spoke first, but she finished his sentence.

"That was..."

"...good."

Then a pause.

Then: "Okay," she said, leaping up, "now I really do have to go."

She quickly crossed to where her clothes were piled on a chair and dressed in an instant.

"Wanna have dinner after work?" he asked, stark naked, stubbly, sleepy-eyed, and drained in every sense of the word.

She, on the other hand, except for a remarkable rosy glow emanating from her cheeks that almost seemed to be warming the entire state of California, and a patch of damp bangs plastered to her forehead, looked remarkably ready for the world.

"I can't, sweetie," she said, opening the door and turning toward him as she backed through it, reaching to touch his face, then kissing it. "Bye."

"Bye," he said, watching her body move gracefully down the hallway and disappear around the corner. But then she peeked back around.

"Hey, I almost forgot," she said. "Cynthia sent you an email inviting you to a pretty wild party tomorrow. It's a Second Acts affair, but despite what transpired here, and this was very lovely, I think you should say yes. I'll be there working, and I think the whole thing might be a boon to our careers. A lot of industry people. Not to mention that it's on Ava Dodd Radcliffe's yacht, which obviously must positively leak money. Okay, gotta go."

Seamus stared for a few moments at the spot from which Paloma had vanished, before closing the door and flopping onto his back on the bed. He lifted his phone to his face and scrolled through his emails. He opened the one from Cynthia and RSVP'd. He picked up the hotel phone and ordered a huge breakfast. Then he showered and put on a plush white robe. He luxuriated while he ate, read the complimentary *New York Times* from front to back, and then headed to the lobby to check out at exactly 12:41 PM.

"Hello," he said to the young man behind the counter, handing over the key. "I need to pay up."

"Very good, sir," the hotel guy replied, "I trust you enjoyed your stay."

"The understatement of the bloody millennium," said Seamus. "Thanks."

"Good, good," said the kid, looking at the screen. "But I'm afraid I have to charge you for two days, since you're forty minutes past check-out."

"Oh, no problem at all," said Seamus, in a tone that seemed like he hadn't a money care in the world. He had the air of a Hollywood player, rather than an unemployed recent arrival, crashing on his brother's couch. "It's well worth it."

"Very well. Do you want to just charge the American

Express card we have on file from last night, Mr. Ramsey?"

"Abso-bloomin'-lutely," replied Seamus with a cat-eating-canary grin.

The hotel kid printed out the itemized bill: $1,259.42. "Please give me your John Hancock," said the kid.

"We don't use that expression in my country," said Seamus, pretending to look over the math, as if he cared in the slightest, "so, I'll give you my John Patrick Clancy O'Shaughnessy O'Brother-this-is-a-long-stinking-name O'Hancock instead. Oh, by the way, I didn't have any small bills for the maid...I guess I'll just add a tip here. Can you see that she gets it?"

"Certainly, sir."

Seamus leaned down, added $400, and signed Max's name with a flourish.

"There you go," he said.

"Oh, my...very generous," said the kid. "She will be very pleased. I hope to see you again too."

"Without a doubt," said Seamus walking on air into the perpetual Los Angeles sunshine.

He didn't have a car. He had seven dollars and thirty-two cents in his pocket. There was a little more cash back at his brother's, but that wasn't going to help him get there from West Hollywood. He wasn't sure if Hollywood cab drivers took credit cards and he didn't want to have the guy wait downstairs while he fetched the money because he didn't want to spend it anyway. He was also sick of cabs, having spent the last ten miserable years in one.

So he checked the map on his phone and set off on foot, up the hill on Alta Loma Road to Sunset Boulevard. He scrolled through a Los Angeles tourism site and decided this was much better anyway. He would pass through Sunset Strip, see the huge statue of Bullwinkle the Moose, still there from back when that show was in production fifty years ago. The Chateau Marmont, tons of billboards selling the latest movies and TV shows...the whole trek was a great introduction to his new town, the town he'd make his own.

He switched over to Hollywood Boulevard to take in the Chinese Theater and the hokey Hollywood hoopla that he'd only seen in books and magazines. He walked slowly, reading the names on the stars in the sidewalk along the way. The Kinks song about Hollywood Boulevard ran through his head and he noticed the occasional name of a fellow Irishman or woman: Barry Fitzgerald, Maureen O'Hara...he wasn't sure if any of the newer ones had made it yet, like Liam Neeson and Colin Farrell. He knew they'd get one if they hadn't yet. He looked at the blank squares, imagining his name in them. He nearly crashed into a huge dingy SpongeBob and then had his picture taken with a scrawny Wonder Woman who did not come close to filling out her costume and was smoking a cigarette and talking out of the side of her mouth like Jimmy Cagney. More like "kinda make you wonder, woman," he thought.

He loved it all: the glitz *and* the grit. Despite the wildly contradictory nature of the place, he felt its powerful seductiveness. He was fully aware of the long-shot nature of pursuing the Hollywood dream, but he didn't care about that. At all. It was what he now knew he wanted more than anything he'd ever wanted.

As much as Paloma enchanted him, as he walked the four-and-a-half miles, he realized Tinsel Town enchanted him too. This yacht bash was something so out of the realm of his experience. It seemed sort of like signing up to be part of some over-privileged woman's fantasy. Actually, it seemed *exactly* like that. But when you added the siren song of Hollywood fame and glory, it was a small price to pay. Being flirted with and fondled by a bunch of beautiful people was a dirty job but somebody had to do it. After all, Paloma would be there and they could surely sneak off and grab some quality time down in the lower deck.

God *knows I love her lower deck,* he thought, smiling to himself. He stopped in his tracks. *I love* all *her decks. I think I love her.*

Chapter 19

FRIDAY 1:30 PM

Max, the man, was rudely awakened when three tongues, ranging from unusually tiny to freakishly large, licked him hard in the face. He was simultaneously being French kissed, having his ear wax cleaned out, and his eyelids pried open to gain slobber access to his eyeballs.

"Wait, what...hold it, hold it!" he said, spitting and clamping his lids tighter than ever. "Hold it!"

Lolita was standing in the middle of her living room, laughing. She had already been awakened by the dogs and then sort of sicced them on Max, urging them to wake him up by any means necessary. Thwarted from licking, Max the Irish wolfhound, started thwacking Max the man across the head with his tail. Max the man was lucky it wasn't King, the Great Dane, whose tail had basically zero fur padding and was as strong as a python.

"Okay!" said Max, struggling to his feet and starting to laugh too. "I get it. You're back!"

He and Lolita had been out looking for the dogs all night. They had reported them missing to the Beverly Hills police, the Los Angeles Police, the Santa Monica Police, and every dog pound within a fifty-mile radius. They finally gave it a rest for the night and had fallen asleep only an hour or so earlier.

And after all that, the three very special canines had just walked right in and sat right down, as if they hadn't nearly driven their ever-loving mama out of her mind.

"Can you believe it?" she asked.

"As a matter of fact, I can," he said. "Where do you think they've been?"

"I don't know, but Wilfredo (the Chihahua) brought me this."

She held out a thick stack of twenty-dollar bills, a bit drooly and dented with teeth marks.

"What the hell," said Max the man. "I guess that's one way to make a living. You could be Fagin to Wilfredo's Artful

Dodger."

She waved bills in the air and put on her best Cockney accent. "You've got to pick a pocket or two, I suppose," she said. "And I wouldn't begin to know how to find out who it belongs to."

"Impossible," he said. "Plus, I could use a little cash. You wanna split it?"

"Tell you what," said Lolita, counting the bills. "You can have a hundred. After all, Wilfredo is *my* Artful Dodger."

"Deal," he said, grabbing his wallet from his pants pocket. "All I've got is a little leftover Irish funny money." He slid the cash in. "Hold on," he said, pulling out his credit cards and license and various other plastic, one by one. "I think I've lost my AmEx. Jesus."

"Are you sure?" asked Lolita. "Do you remember where you used it last?"

"Well, it had to be in Dublin. I haven't used it here yet. I used a different card at the Miramar."

He immediately called AmEx and found out that the card had seen action four times in the past ten hours in four separate spots in Hollywood——a bar on Pico, a restaurant on La Cienega, of course the Sunset Marquis Hotel, and Madame Tussaud's Wax Museum on Hollywood Boulevard.

"Wait," said Max. "Sounds like I was pickpocketed by a tourist. Isn't that the exact *opposite* of what's supposed to happen?"

"Yes, that's right, sir. So, you are sure it wasn't you who signed at the Sunset Marquis?" asked the woman.

"Yes!" said Max. "How could I not be sure of that?"

"You'd be surprised, sir."

"Okay, yeah. Well, I am. Sure. I haven't been to the Sunset Marquis in ten years."

"All right, then. So, I guess it goes without saying that it wasn't you who gave the maid a four hundred-dollar tip and included a handwritten note next to it that says...hold on, let me blow it up on the screen. Yes, let's see, 'For the maid, of course, but more importantly as a massive 'f-word' you to a world-class a-hole named Max.'"

"No," said Max, shaking his head. "That was not me."

Chapter 20

FRIDAY 1:42 PM

By the time Seamus made it back to Los Feliz, his feet were sore and he was feeling a bit dizzy. Dizzy from exercise, dehydration, love, and Hollywood dreams.

He stopped off at a local grocery store to pick up a soda, but when he got in there, it occurred to him that he should probably buy some food for his big brother's refrigerator...be a good house guest and all that. So, he filled a shopping cart to the brim, with meat and vegetables and desserts and wine and beer and anything else that looked good.

He waited in a very long line. So he was of course quite disappointed when he was told that his American Express card had been declined.

It was embarrassing, to be sure, but even more than that it was a crushing end to his Hollywood fantasy of opulence. He felt dejected and very, very poor.

He turned to walk away and then stopped. He looked in his wallet again. "Excuse me, Miss," he said to the heavily pierced cashier, "Is there a Starbucks anywhere around here?"

She looked at him like he was a moron. "There's a Starbucks everywhere around here. Walking in any direction."

"Thank you kindly," he said over his shoulder.

He found a Starbucks in twenty-seven seconds.

"Can I help you," asked the cheerful Starbucks lady.

"Yes, you may," he said, taking the card out of his wallet, "I seem to have lost track. Could you tell me how much I've got left on here?"

She swiped it. "Oh, my. You have six hundred and twenty-one dollars and thirty-seven cents. I didn't even know they came that high."

"Right," said Seamus, beyond amazed. "That's just about what I thought. It was a gift from Mr. Starbucks himself."

"Uhh...I'm pretty sure there is no Mr. Starbucks."

"Oh, I know, I was pulling your leg. Okay, I'll tell you what, I'll take all the food in that case. Every bit of it. All the pastries, all the sandwiches, the fruit, the yogurt with the fruit with the little crumbly granola bits on top, all of 'em."

"Are you kidding?" she asked, her eyes wide, starting to ring stuff up. Two other people starting bagging.

"Not kidding. I am very hungry. Famished. I haven't eaten in ages. Also throw in all the cookies and graham crackers with the chocolate and all those little bags of nuts. Okay, let's see where we're at."

The line was growing behind him and people started whispering that he was hogging everything.

"You can't buy it *all*, asshole," said a scowling, slick businessman in the back of the line. His arms were crossed and he was tapping his foot like a lunatic. "Maybe that's what they do back in *England*..."

"Hold on, Slick," said Seamus. "Did you say *England?*"

"He's obviously *Irish*," said the young woman next to Seamus. "But still, it's totally rude."

"We have more in back," said the cashier.

"What an asshole," said Slick.

"She just said they have more in the back," said the young woman in line. "I think it's kind of funny that he's buying all this stuff."

"Oh, yeah?" said Slick. "Well, you're a jerk too then."

"Slick!" said Seamus. "You're not listening. They have more in back. Let's just see the tally."

The barista finished swiping. There were mountains of paper sacks all over the counter, on top of the case, and on the floor. "You've still got eighty-three dollars and eleven cents left," she said.

"Okay, tell you what," said Seamus, "I really only want five or six bags anyway. Everybody else split up the rest and then finish up the card for whatever else you want."

A loud cheer went up among the previously pissed-off coffee lovers.

"Except, nothing for Slick," said Seamus, picking out a few sacks and walking out.

#

"Seamus!" called Donald over the roar of the cappuccino machine, "Where the hell have you been?"

"Nowhere special," he said, saddling up to the coffee bar and depositing the sacks of goodies, "just out making significant headway toward fame, fortune, and the pursuit of fucking happiness, that's all."

"Jesus, what the feck are you doin' with the devil's shite? In case you didn't notice I *own* a feckin' coffee shop?"

"I know, Donald, I know. And I'm sorry. I was just walking down the road, minding my own business, when I just got awful hungry all of a sudden. I couldn't help myself."

"Jesus, well take this shite upstairs," looking through the booty. "I can't have people seeing it around my place! But let me just take one of these graham crackers with the chocolate. I love those."

Chapter 21

FRIDAY 5:45 PM

"T.G.I.F., Paloma" said Cynthia, turning off her computer and rubbing her eyes. "I kind of wish it were already M."

"Yeah, but we're in good shape," she replied. "Every date is on track. Nobody's sick, no last minute cancelations...all systems go."

"Let's run through it one more time. By the way, do you want to go to that opening at LACMA with me? It might be nice for you to meet Ava. Plus the art is kind of amazing."

"Yes! I was hoping you'd ask. Don't we need to get going, though?"

"Oh, we've got time," said Cynthia. "It starts at seven, but it goes 'til ten. We can be fashionably late. It'll be good for us to be together to confer if any client emergencies arise."

"Okay, so, date one," said Paloma, looking at her iPad. **Johnny and Lalin. John Tabor,** up and coming art director in movies. Loves rock music and travel. Has been around the world multiple times. **Lalin Mariso,** transplant from Argentina. Novelist...her first book comes out in a month. Daughter of a famous Argentinian dissident. Cosmopolitan, yet hasn't traveled much herself. But really, really wants to. If this isn't a match, I will eat my hat. I'll eat *your* hat too."

"I agree," said Cynthia. "As you see, I've tweaked one of their date destinations a bit. There's a bar in Santa Monica called Vagabond. The whole place is dedicated to the romance of travel. The ancient walls are covered with photos and stickers from around the world, sort of like an old-fashioned steamer trunk. You wouldn't believe it. I'm amazed the place can keep *any* customers...it makes you want to pay up fast and drive to the airport. If these two don't stumble out of there with airline reservations purchased via their iPhones, I'll eat an entire millinery shop."

"Brilliant," said Paloma, truly in awe.

"Okay, let's continue," said Cynthia.

"**Will Algren,** fashion photographer...matched with **Nadine Ulmante.** Beautiful enough to be a fashion model——in fact, she did it for a while in her teens——but now is a painter. She shows in galleries across the states and Europe."

"Perfect," said Cynthia. "What would have been a busman's holiday is instead a match made in heaven."

"**Magda Carpenter,** an acting coach, matched with **Davis MacGregor,** a surgeon. Big egos, obviously. And he acted in college, so that could have been dicey. But, as you know, she is a middle child to his first-born. She's a diplomat. Patient. A calming influence on his majesty. Boss, you are a genius."

"Thanks," said Cynthia, "although the birth-order thing is by no means an exact science. Did you happen to notice anything else in their bios that would portend well?"

"Hold on, hold on...they share the same all-time favorite movie: *Some Like it Hot*. Both have seen it dozens of times."

"Exactly! I predict wedding bells in six months. Next!"

"**Allen Schiller,** a creator of animated cartoons. He's funny and charming and bursting with creativity. Matched with **Alana Marwen,** a jewelry designer. She just got a huge commission to supply her work with a major department store chain. Both creative, but in different fields. Zero competition, mutual admiration. Both sexy as hell."

"Love them. I switched them out from the hotel I'd penciled in first, though. I booked them in Artists' Retreat in Santa Barbara. Have you heard of it? Deluxe, lovely cabins in the woods, but high above the town, with a sweeping view of the ocean. Every cabin has a separate studio with drawing tables, art supplies, and a concrete floor you don't have to worry about messing up. In fact, you're encouraged to mess it up. I'd be surprised if they *ever* check out."

"Good God," said Paloma, "I want to *live* there."

"Okay, but please don't leave me right away. Who's the fifth again?"

"**Darius Carlotta,** an award-winning documentary filmmaker, who you paired with **Tara Beckwith,** an elementary school teacher, turned politician, turned stripper, turned poet. And singer. Oh, and songwriter. She's writing a freaking opera."

"I know," said Cynthia. "This Beckwith woman is a walking-talking subject of a documentary film. Turn on the camera, Darius...the film makes itself! God *damn*, I'm good, Ms. Rodriguez," she continued, giggling slightly and then bursting into all-out laughter.

"The only question is whether they get married or win an Oscar first," said Paloma, laughing very hard now too. "I just hope we get invited to the premiere *and* the wedding."

They were nearly hysterical for a few minutes, laughing and crying. It was the kind of laughter you get from being over-tired, over-stressed, and just really needing and wanting to lose control for a bit.

"Okay," said Cynthia wiping away a mirth-induced tear, "let's get over to the museum.

"Okay, Boss," said Paloma, standing up and sighing out a few more giggles. "My face hurts. How do you do this?"

"It's all about putting the right characters into the right story."

"Genius," said Paloma.

Cynthia was beginning to really appreciate Paloma.

Paloma could imagine staying in this job forever if it weren't for the fact that she really did want to be a famous actress. And that was definitely one cold, hard, undeniable, certifiable, carved-in-stone, irreversible fact.

Chapter 22

Pete Blatt got up remarkably early this sunny Saturday morning in Kyoto. The day before had been a travel day, so he had actually gotten to bed at a relatively reasonable hour. The other band mates had headed out to paint the town, but he'd declined. His plan was to get up early and call Cynthia at a halfway normal hour for California and he'd aimed for a time that seemed right: after her regular office hours, but before the evening date-night phone traffic began.

So he had the idea of getting out early and heading for the Daikaku-ji Temple. This place was seriously ancient. It was established in 876. It's located adjacent to the Ozawa pond and the Heian era garden...among the oldest gardens in Kyoto.

He thought it would be a good place to find a little peace and then bring that peace to his conversation with Cynthia. He was calling just to talk. To explain the last disastrous phone call, as much as he could explain, because he'd been groggy enough at the time to seriously impair his ability to establish a firm recollection. He'd been a mess, he knew that much.

He arrived at the temple and walked around for a while. He came to a strange grotto and sat down. He wasn't terribly spiritual, but this place would inspire that tendency in the most committed atheist. He was feeling the best he'd felt in weeks. Clear headed, focused, ready to connect.

He called Cynthia.

She was driving down Vermont through Korea Town on her way to LACMA. The traffic was heavy, the neighborhood dense with electric weekend bustle. Paloma was riding shotgun and controlling the music, which was now blaring some weird soul-rap concoction that included violins, a full church choir, and a rhythm section that seemed to be made up mostly of gunfire. Cynthia had no idea who or what it was, but she loved it.

Her phone rang.

She looked down and saw that it was Pete.

She did not pick up.

Chapter 23

The museum was seriously hopping. Some kind of sexy funk was booming, making the whole affair seem quite un-museum-like. Ava was being swarmed by admirers...an exclusive crowd of artists, collectors, movie folk, household names, and the very richest denizens of Los Angeles.

When Cynthia walked in, under those massive iron tits, the first thing she wondered was why Ava needed any help at all in the dating department. She was surrounded by enough gorgeous flesh to satisfy the appetites of an army of rich widows. The next thing Cynthia noticed was the absurdly handsome man standing to Ava's left. She couldn't believe he was here, but, then again, it made perfect sense. Why wouldn't he be?

Jack Stone. The movie star. The movie star who Cynthia had almost fallen for, or rather who had spun a web that she had nearly gotten trapped in.

Good God.

She grabbed Paloma by the arm and forced her to take a hard right toward the bar.

"Hey, look," said the younger woman, "isn't that…"

"No, I mean yes," whispered Cynthia. "I need a drink."

"Oh, okay," said Paloma. "I mean hell yes, Boss."

They got in the booze line and almost instantly someone touched Cynthia's shoulder, making her jump slightly.

"Miss Amas, I presume." No mistaking that movie star voice.

Paloma had heard something about Cynthia's Jack Stone adventure…how he had come to her for help with his love life——a notion so absurd on its face, that Cynthia couldn't believe she had ever fallen for it. Of course, he had pursued her instead. But Paloma didn't know anything about the ugly, bloody, funny fiasco with Jack, Max, Lolita, and mega Hollywood director Steven Sternberg. Plus Sternberg's wife. And, worst of all, their daughter.

"Well, of course you're here," said Cynthia——thinking,

Could this weekend get any more ridiculous?——while shaking his hand. "Jack, this is Paloma. Paloma, Jack. Oh, and Jack? Keep your hands off Paloma."

"Cynthia," he said with the innocence of a newborn lamb in wolf's clothing, "I'm just shaking her hand."

"Yeah," she replied, "but with you shaking hands is a gateway drug."

Paloma and Jack both laughed nervously. Jack was amused, while Paloma seemed slightly irritated.

"I've shaken men's hands before, you know," she replied, sounding a little perturbed.

Jack looked Paloma in the eye, holding both of her hands in both of his. "Cynthia's been in the dating industry too long. She has a dirty mind. Let me get you both a drink."

Even though they were still four people away from the front of the line, as soon as he turned toward the bar, one of the young women in a white shirt and black vest, smiled at him and said, "Can I get you something, Mr. Stone?"

In normal circumstances——say in a real-life bar with mostly real-life people——this kind of line cutting would have led to a major brouhaha. There would have been some version of, "Hey, what the hell?!! Who do you think you are?!!" But everyone knew very well who he was and they were more intoxicated by his close proximity than they'd be from the wine they were waiting for.

"Oh, my," said Jack looking around at the other art lovers in the cue, "I had no intention of cutting ahead. Please, no. These people are next."

But *these people* objected. "No, no! Go right ahead, Mr. Stone." "No problem at all." "Here, scooch over, let him in. C'mon, scooch!"

"Oh, jeez, thanks, everyone," he said, patting one thrilled older woman on the back as he passed. "Just three Cabernets I guess. Is that right, girls?" He turned back to look at Cynthia and Paloma.

"Yes, thanks," they said in unison, both somewhat mortified.

When he returned with the drinks, Cynthia said, "Thanks," but immediately turned from Jack, leading Paloma in the other direction. "I should really introduce Paloma to Ava."

"Yes, of course," said Jack. "Exactly what I was going to say. Besides, I see Broderick Patton over there all alone and I should really go say hello."

Broderick Patton was the newest young soon-to-be superstar in town. Paloma almost got whiplash turning to see him as Cynthia yanked her in the other direction. She had just seen him in *Before the Revolution*, and he had blown her away.

"We're here to work, Paloma," she said, smiling and rolling her eyes.

"I know, I know," she replied, "but come on, poor Broderick Patton is all alone."

"Yeah, right," said Cynthia. "Poor baby. Well, he can commiserate with Jack about the pitiful hands life has dealt them."

Cynthia and Paloma moved through the tightly packed gallery, zigzagging through movers and shakers and mover-shaker watchers and wannabes.

"Hello, Ava," said Cynthia when she finally penetrated her ring of admirers. "The show is incredible."

"Cynthia, my dear," she whispered, raising her wine glass and backing away from the others, "thank you so much for coming." She clearly wanted to keep their conversation private. She also sounded like this was far from her first glass of wine.

"Wouldn't miss it," said Cynthia. "This is Paloma. She's coming along on the Que Sera Sarong voyage."

"Wonderful," said Ava, reaching for Paloma's hand. "I can see why she chose you. You're gorgeous."

"Oh, no," said Cynthia, nearly spit-taking cabernet across

the room, "Paloma is my assistant."

"Oh!" laughed Ava. "So sorry, my mistake. Very sorry."

"No reason to apologize," said Paloma, blushing slightly and smiling a sweet closed-mouth smile as she shook Ava's hand. "If I weren't working that night, I'd be happy to attend."

They all laughed, clinked glasses, and took sips of wine.

"Oh, the other thing, Cynthia," murmured Ava, "I hope we're not at capacity already, because I've invited a couple of others."

Cynthia was almost sure she knew one of the names before she heard it. She was going to say, *Hey, I thought everyone is supposed to be strangers*, but then she figured, what the heck, it's Ava's fantasy, let her define it.

"I've invited Jack Stone, who I understand you already know. Also...an old friend of mine and Jonathon who you definitely would *not* know. I'll email you his info. He suddenly finds himself single and up for adventure."

Well, actually, Ava, we do have a full house, I mean ship, said Cynthia to herself, while nodding in agreement.

Then her phone *plinked* and she looked down to see a text from Johnny Tabor, the art director with wanderlust...the one on the date with Lalin Mariso.

Cynthia, Paloma-

Just leaving Vagabond. Bad news... cutting date short. Cancelled restaurant. Good news: driving to LAX. Not sure where headed. Will decide when we get to int terminal. Thanks for everything and bon voyage, Johnny and Lalin.

Cynthia blurted out a small, but joyous, laugh. "Apparently wanderlust plus wanderlust equals wandering plain-old lust," she said, holding the phone up for Paloma and Ava to see.

"My goodness, you are good," said Ava.

"Speaking of good," said Paloma, pointing to a large pink and beige canvas, "there's some art that just plain feels good."

The canvas depicted, in extreme close-up, an epic bird's-eye view of a something...a landscape...an architectural foundation? It was all angles and almost abstract. But then... oh, right...open legs around closed legs, two triangles of pubic hair united to create an hourglass shape, pubic bones merged, and *bone submerged*...the deepest point of male and female sexual congress, cropped in tight. It was at once clinical, like a diagram of plumbing or a male-female electrical plug, but also highly erotic, recalling that moment of impact in the minds and loins of onlookers.

"I know," said Ava. "That painting made me hot before

I realized why. I was meditating on it when I decided to contact you, Cynthia."

They all laughed and clinked glasses again.

Cynthia heard another *plink* and looked down to see a text from Lolita.

How's the opening? It sure would have been nice to know about it. No big deal…I guess you'd rather go with your employee. What's her name? Pauline or Paulina or something? Never mind. I'll see you tomorrow in Long Beach. I'd ask if you'd like to drive down together, but you'd probably rather go with that Pauline or Paulina or whatever. OK, see you tomorrow. - Lo

Cynthia shook her head. How on Earth did Lolita even know she was there? Maybe she'd told her. What did she have against Paloma all of a sudden? She got another text, this one from Magda Carpenter, the acting coach:

Cynthia: Things were going fine until we left the restaurant. We were walking toward the valet, when the high heel of my left shoe snapped. Over I went and I sprained my ankle pretty badly. I thought it was broken, but Davis——an orthopedic surgeon——knew it wasn't. He carried me to the car. He's in the pharmacy right now buying ace bandages and writing me a prescription for Percocet. I never knew excruciating pain could be so romantic.

Well, I could have told her that, thought Cynthia.

Oh, here he comes. Hey, BTW, have you ever made love under the influence of narcotics? I mean I'm not positive we're headed there, but it's beginning to seem pretty likely. When it numbs away the pain does it numb all feeling? Everywhere?

Despite the madness, these matches just keep working like magic.

But Cynthia also saw that she had three or four texts from Pete. She couldn't ignore him forever.

Cynthia: I miss you. I really need to talk. Call me. I've cleared my morning. I am waiting.

– Pete

"Ava? Paloma? I really need to find a quiet place to make a call. Would you excuse me for a moment?"

"Of course," said Ava, still whispering. "I'll introduce the young Paloma to some of my stuffy old rich birds and bird-ettes. She can see first hand that although money can't buy happiness, it can certainly buy boredom."

Ouch. Cynthia *had* noticed that most of the younger

people who had been in Ava's vicinity when she and Paloma first arrived, had now dispersed throughout the room, leaving mostly old-fogeys and middle-aged-fogeys behind. In any case, it seemed like Ava had said that thing about boredom a little too loudly.

Cynthia headed back out between and under the two titanic boobs. A young artist or artist impersonator was having his picture taken in front of one of the breasts. He was standing on his tiptoes, reaching in vain toward the nipple, still at least fifteen feet out of his reach. He kept trying different poses, arms outstretched, pretending to try to encircle the orb with them. It was like when people have their photos taken attempting to hug a giant redwood tree, their tiny arms absurdly inadequate to take it all in. His cute girlfriend was taking the pictures and giggling at every new antic.

Cynthia headed down the hallway and out into the courtyard, sipping her wine along the way. It was still pretty loud, since there was another bar out there.

She saw someone she knew at the far corner of the plaza: Molly Hannigan, the ex-wife of Steven Sternberg, perhaps the most famous producer-director on this particular planet. Cynthia and Lolita had been there the day they'd broken up.

So had Max Ramsey, Jack Stone, and dozens of friends and associates. It all came down on their picture-perfect, ocean-view, Pacific Palisades estate, when an avalanche of dirty, dark revelations rained down upon them for all to see. Many others had a role in the circumstances that eventually led to their horrifically messy divorce, but Jack Stone and Max were by far the most culpable. The number of lies and betrayals involved were nearly incomprehensible. The casualties were numerous. It was an eventful afternoon, marking the end of the world as they knew it...the end of many things: one marriage, at least four affairs, friendships, parent-child relationships, and one of the more successful collaborations in recent Hollywood history. Jack and Sternberg, best friends and colleagues for decades, were still not speaking to each other. Jack's career had taken a major hit. Three important projects instantly went up in smoke when Sternberg discovered that his best friend Jack was a far, far more *intimate* friend of his wife, Molly.

Jack had since become a bit of a caricature of himself, his lies and duplicitous shenanigans now so widely reported, so transparent, so public, that for the first time in twenty years he was having trouble convincing young starlets to be as star-struck and stupid as he had come to depend on them to be in order to keep his revolving harem fresh.

Sternberg had announced his retirement from movies. In addition to everything else, he'd been working on a Broadway musical at the time——*Gambling Rose*, based on the plight of Pete Rose, the disgraced baseball star——so he immediately picked up and moved to New York in time for the premiere. The highly anticipated production, starring Matt Damon as Rose, had cost ninety-two million dollars to stage. It closed in three days: "Rose Pops Up, Poops Out"——*Variety*. "Rose Blooms, Withers and Dies"——*New York Times*. "Rose Inducted into Hall of Theatrical Shame"——Time Out "Sternberg Gambles, Loses"——*Wall Street Journal*.

Molly had gone off the deep end. She'd been cheating on Sternberg with Jack Stone *and* Max (separately, not together) and, even worse, her daughter Mariana was also screwing Jack Stone and was in fact deeply in love with him. The cherry on top of this disastrously incestuous parfait was that although Molly was shockingly unconcerned about losing Steven and Jack——other than harboring a certain lingering affection for Steven's massive fortune and Jack's similarly oversized instrument of love (one not-small detail that did make one wonder whether Molly were in the vicinity tonight because *Jack* was)——she was still deeply, desperately, some say stark-raving-madly in love with Max. It was non-reciprocal. As in restraining-order non-reciprocal.

Since that fateful day, she had been arrested no less than three times for accosting Max and/or causing a public nuisance wherever he happened to be, which required tenacity, because he had not had a regular address in quite a while, preferring instead to bounce around from nice to nicer hotels. Incident one: she appeared out of nowhere nearly naked in a dressing room in the men's department of Barneys New York in Beverly Hills. Incident two: on the beach at Hotel del Coronado, wearing only hot pants, an enormous straw hat, and a child's inflatable plastic tube around her chest like a bikini top. And incident three, weirdest of all: outside Arclight Cinema, greeting him after a Sunday matinee, wearing only a raincoat, a martini, and a small loaded pistol. No shots were fired, but that was the incident that led to the restraining order. Max was with a date at the time, so even though he felt bad about taking legal action, he was more afraid for the safety of the other women in his life than for himself.

Molly spent some time in rehab in Malibu and had just recently rejoined society, but the order was still in effect. She was not to get within two hundred yards of Max.

Mariana, the daughter, had moved to England to write a

tell-all book about the family and was not on speaking terms with anyone *in the family.*

Incredibly, the whole thing was a big positive for Cynthia. She narrowly escaped being but another fly stuck in Jack's worldwide spider web, and even more importantly, had finally broken free from the disastrously toxic charms of Max Ramsey, who had been a fun but ultimately bad recurring habit of hers for years.

Cynthia squinted in Molly's direction. She was talking with friends, drinking wine...which was maybe a bad sign. On the other hand, she was wearing designer something or other and not a Hula Hoop, so that was a relatively *good* sign. She actually looked okay...professionally coifed, put together. Cynthia detected a certain nervous energy, but Molly had always been a bit high strung. Bird-like. Poodle-like. You get the picture.

Cynthia wandered further and finally found a quiet spot on a bench in the Rodin sculpture garden...ironic since it had a similar ambience to the Kyoto garden from which Pete had called her. Except these Rodins had the added component of muscularity and sensuality...titanic figures stretching and straining bigger-than-life angst and passion . . . raging against the mundane, the routine, the complacent...the distant and removed: in other words, her current so-called relationship with Pete.

She pressed call.

But Pete had gotten up incredibly early, especially for a musician, and when he couldn't reach Cynthia, he'd retreated to the hotel. Determined to stay awake, he'd made coffee, read the paper, watched TV news, and noodled around on the guitar a bit. But despite his best efforts, he drifted into dreamland, this time with a vengeance. Maybe he was dreaming about having a girlfriend less than ten time zones away, maybe not. In any case, even though he'd held his phone in his hand to make sure that if Cynthia called it would wake him, it didn't. He responded exactly like a dead man. Or, as it appeared to Cynthia, an uncaring, unavailable, or non-existent boyfriend.

The phone rang ten times and then Cynthia was bounced to voicemail. She could not believe it. This was beyond ridiculous. Pete had been on the road for twelve weeks and although they had at least started off with a fairly hot and heavy long-distance thing, now even that had fallen apart, as if the connection had gotten lost somewhere halfway across the Pacific Ocean, en route from a distant satellite, or stranded at a fried cell tower. It wasn't very long ago that it seemed like all systems were go with Cynthia and Pete and now it felt like all systems were going, going, gone. And there still was no clear end date for the tour. Every time they played a concert, they added another one on at the end. It seemed endless. Even his voicemail message irritated her now. She'd heard it a million times before, but today it got under her skin:

"Hi, you've reached Pete. Well, you've reached Pete's phone. Talk to Pete's phone, Pete's phone will talk to Pete, and then Pete will talk to your phone. *Beep!*"

The first time, actually the first ten or so times, she'd heard that message, she'd laughed. But now it wasn't funny at all... just an accurate description of their life. She left a very short message:

"Hi, Pete's phone. Say goodbye to Pete for me."

She headed back along the garden path, cursing the fact that the emotions conveyed by the Rodin sculptures were so much more vital than her own frustration, impotence, and numbing dissatisfaction.

She gulped down the last bit of wine and threw it against

a rough-hewn marble wall, like throwing a champagne glass into a fireplace. But the plastic "glass" just bounced off. Even her drama had no drama.

As she climbed the steps and entered the courtyard, she decided to head over to the ladies' room. She ducked into a deserted corridor. These particular restrooms were off the beaten path, not the main ones close to the action where the opening was taking place, which would undoubtedly have long lines.

Her phone buzzed and she looked down to see that it was Darius Carlotta, the documentary filmmaker who was out on a date with Tara Beckwith, the most fascinating woman in the world.

"Hi Cynthia. Listen, I've just gotta tell you that you are a genius. A relationship genius. I have never had a date this perfect. Just wanted to say thanks. –Darius

Yeah, I'm a relationship genius all right.

She pushed into the ladies' room door, but it didn't move. At first she assumed it was just locked and not available this evening. But then she heard sounds from inside...two people...a man and a woman. She put her ear to the door, but she couldn't hear much until a female voice said very distinctly, "OH, JACK."

Good God. Obviously a Jack Stone/Molly Hannigan reunion going on in there.

She thought about banging on the door and breaking it up. But Jack was Ava's friend. Plus, what could she do, tell them they had to stop? They were consenting adults. Consenting adults with more than a few screws maybe, but still. She worried about Molly, but it was her life. Cynthia used the men's room instead.

Back in the gallery, Cynthia looked for Paloma and Ava, but ended up talking with Anton somebody, one of the artists. He had created an x-rated totem pole, covered with lip prints, rising twenty feet upward and culminating in a huge, bulging man-penis head. It was even more obscene than one would imagine from that obscene description. Anton was a lovely man and incredibly handsome. Under the circumstances——the Pete call, the restroom incident——Cynthia was happy to have someone to flirt with. But unfortunately, just when their repartee was getting good, another ridiculously handsome man approached and said to Anton, "Okay, Sweetie, time to go home."

Cynthia mingled for a while.

Chapter 24

FRIDAY 10:11 PM

"Jack," said Paloma, holding her fingers to his lips, "I'm really not up for this. I need to get back out there."

"Oh, come on."

"I met someone," she said.

"What, since yesterday? Since we talked about hooking up here?"

"Yes, as a matter of fact."

"Really, Paloma? Well, what does that have to do with it? I assume you're not *married* or anything. I hope to God you didn't marry this new someone within minutes of meeting him."

"No, of course not," she replied. "Okay, listen, this is the last time for a while. Maybe forever. I'm tired of it."

"You're tired of what?"

"This. It's just not working for me anymore."

He knew this day would come. He didn't know that she had wanted to end their affair *before* she even *met* Seamus. In fact, much earlier than that...before Jack let her know that he'd heard Cynthia was looking for an assistant. When Cynthia hired Paloma, she and Jack agreed their affair was better kept secret from Cynthia.

"Okay, all right," he whispered, unbuttoning her white blouse, revealing exquisite mocha skin. He slipped the bra strap from her shoulder, kissed the place where it had been, and left a long row of kisses en route to her breast. He held her in his arms, slid his powerful hands under her perfect bottom, and eased her up onto the counter, her legs encircling him, her skirt hiked up near her waist.

"But if it's going to be the last time," he continued, getting closer——lips gently brushing lips, mouths trading warm breaths——"let's make it special." He hooked an index finger around the elastic waistband of her purple undies and began to ease them off.

"Right," she said in a devastating deadpan. "Because what's more special than a public restroom?"

He stopped. It was like she'd pressed a "pause" button. They just looked at each other.

"You know," she said, placing her hand on the hand that was pulling off her panties, "I changed my mind. I gotta go." She rearranged her lingerie and closed her blouse.

"Wait, no...Paloma. Why are you doing this? Our last time was our most glorious love-making ever."

"It was okay," said Paloma, sounding distant, sliding onto her feet.

"Okay?" asked Jack.

"Yeah, whatever, it was great," she said, re-buttoning, no longer making eye contact. "But that first time in Mexico will always stand out for me."

"Oh, well, yeah," he said, gazing into the bathroom mirror, wishing he could see into the past. "You'd just turned twenty-one. You came along with your mother. I was on that war movie."

"Right, *The Final Battle*," she said, staring at him like he was mentally deficient. "I know. I was there."

Despite Paloma's maturity and intelligence, today, with Jack, she sounded like a teenager. Then again, so did he.

"Listen, Paloma, are you sure about this?" He used the movie-star tone and megawatt smile that always made her melt.

Except today. She didn't even seem to notice. She checked the mirror, combed her bangs with her fingers, applied a quick lip-gloss touch-up, and finally looked at him.

"Speaking of 'sure,' Jack, are you sure that on that fateful day in Mexico I had really turned twenty-one?"

Jack stopped smiling. He opened his mouth as if to say something, but nothing came out.

"I'm kidding," giggled Paloma, rolling her eyes.

Chapter 25

Lolita returned home from an evening of shopping. Max had some kind of major meeting on the phone with his Dublin associates, so he'd disappeared, which was fine because she decided she needed some new things for the party. She was standing in front of the full-length mirror in her bedroom, but she wasn't the only one checking out the skintight minidress she was modeling. Her three dogs were lined up like patient boyfriends watching a personal fashion show outside a department store dressing room. The dress's blue and white stripes gave it a certain conservative yacht-clubby feeling, but the stripes also accentuated her topography to such a degree that it conveyed a powerful come-hither-in-a-hurry signal that ninety-nine percent of all sailors everywhere would likely respond to with big, hard salutes. All hands on deck! Hoist the mainsail! Come about! Ahoy, matey!

To tell you the truth, Lolita was getting hot just looking at herself.

And that was the most conservative article of clothing she was bringing along. She was looking forward to it. Max would not be there, which was good. Or maybe not.

Could Max be changing? That moment on the Vespa. The way he's acting. But, come on, Lolita…be serious. This is Max we're talking about.

She called Tanya.

"Hi, Lo," answered her employee, who happened to be reclining on her couch, with her boyfriend, rapper and chess enthusiast Dr. T-bone, at that very moment. Ever since Lolita lured Tanya back to Dog Groomer to the Stars after firing her for having sex with T-Bone at work, their relationship had been much more respectful. Tanya had gotten a big raise and they had both been very accommodating of each other's needs and schedules. This weekend was a good example. In the early days of the shop, Lolita wouldn't even *think* of going away for a weekend. Now, Tanya covered for her and, this weekend, even Dr. T-Bone was coming in to help out.

"Hi, Tanya. Sorry to call so late, but I know you're a night owl, right?"

Dr. T-Bone's tongue flicked across Tanya's ear and she let out a strange little squeal, the result of trying to contain a much larger squeal. She slapped T-Bone on the top of his head.

"Tanya?" asked Lolita, concerned. "Are you all right? You're not crying are you?"

T-Bone flicked and fluttered, double-time.

"No!" she said in an octave that she was pretty sure she had never hit, ever. "Not crying. I'm fine. What's up?"

Another head slap.

"Oh, nothing much. Just checking in, making sure you're all set for tomorrow. It should be kind of busy...lots of pick-ups. Did you ever put that order in for shampoos and stuff?"

Flick, flick, flutter, flutter. Double head slap.

"YES!" shrieked Tanya, losing control and sliding off the couch, onto her shoulders on the floor, her legs up high, and now locked around T-Bone's neck. He looked down at her, smiling.

"Okay, okay!" said Lolita, "I'm not accusing you of forgetting or anything, I just want to make sure."

"I know, Lolita," said Tanya, holding T-Bone's face at bay

with an outstretched palm. "Sorry I over-reacted. I ordered from just about everyone on Wednesday. Grooming stuff, food, toys, dog beds...I did an inventory on Monday, so we'll be in good shape. Are you looking forward to the whole yacht thing?"

"Oh, sure. It'll be fun," said Lolita, looking in the mirror, holding the phone under her neck and adjusting both breasts with her hands. She was trying to decide whether the dress would be better braless.

T-Bone slid over the edge of the couch like a snake slithering toward a runaway mouse. Tanya stuck her arm in T-Bone's face again, her arm pretty much blocking her view of him. She felt his cheeks brushing against her thighs. He pushed harder against her hand, persistently advancing on his prey, the two of them locked in isometric tension.

"Okay, Lolita," she said, her hand now jammed against T-Bone's nose, his tongue out, tasting air. "I've really gotta go. I'm tired and have to get some sleep if I'm going to be at my best in the morning."

"Yes, yes, that's good," replied Lolita, seemingly impressed by her employee's dedication. "I'll let you go then. I still have to pack anyway. Bye-bye."

Tanya released T-Bone's face from her grip and his tongue

reached home as they both finally landed on the colorful coil rug, wedged between the couch and coffee table.

"Number one: do not *ever* do that again!" she said, breathing harder. "Number two: I thought she'd never get off the freaking phone! And three: get your face out of there and make me *really* happy!! Now!"

That was just fine with Dr. T-Bone, who was about to explode unassisted. He scrambled up her body like an excited lizard, stopping ever-so-briefly at her small, perfect breasts——God, *I love you*, he said to them, *but there's no time right now*——before plowing her into the coffee table, sending one half-bottle of Merlot, two glasses, two plates and three containers of Chinese take-out——all that and a bag of chips, literally a bag of chips——onto the floor.

"Good God, yes, yes, yes, motherfucker, holy, yes, goddamn! ARRRGGGHHHH!" said Tanya and T-Bone.

Actually, it was hard to tell who said what. At least it was for Lolita, who hadn't hung up because she was fully aware of what had been going on the entire time and just sort of wanted to listen in. Well, not *sort of*. She was touching her breasts in the mirror the whole time. Somehow her dress ended up scrunched up above her waist, and her underwear, which she had kicked off, landed on Wilfredo's head. He and the other dogs were confused.

What's up with Mommy?

"So sue me," she said.

She gently pressed *End Call*.

Chapter 26

FRIDAY EVENING

"Okay, then," said Max, "Call me as soon as you know."

He'd been talking to his business associates in Dublin on the phone, and speaking very loudly too, but no one cared much because the Coral Tree Cafe on San Vicente was much noisier than a normal coffee shop. It was a surprisingly funky, sprawling space for tony Brentwood. It seemed like a throwback to the hippy days. Nowadays, a patron or two might exude a certain soupçon of ex-hippy, but they'd be as filthy rich as everybody else in there. Max liked it because he could eat, drink coffee, work, and, yes, talk above a whisper on the phone.

He was on the verge of the biggest deal of his life. Max

had never really had trouble making money. He had a lot of specialized skills and a head for business and he hardly ever worked terribly hard. But this was different. If this thing went through he'd never need to work again. He could dedicate himself fulltime to the life of leisure he so richly deserved. He merely wanted to retire early to a civilized existence full of two deadly sins: Lust and Sloth. Was this too much to ask?

"Hi," said Max to the adorable hipster girl behind the counter. "Can I get another refill?"

"Of course, honey pie," she said with a sly smile. "How 'bout another donut with your Joe?"

This twenty-something seemed to have made peace with her minimum wage job by wholly embracing a persona modeled on her idea of a 1950s waitress.

"Is your name Doris? Or Mabel?" asked Max.

"No, sweetie," she giggled, filling up his cup, "the name's Summer Starlight Friedman. I know. My parents were total hippies. I'm going to change it as soon as I leave home. Maybe the next time you see me I *will* be Mabel."

"Ha. You really should have a pack of cigarettes rolled up in your sleeve, you know," he said, taking his coffee and blowing on it.

"Yeah, I know, but I don't smoke. That's where I draw the...

the..."

Suddenly she was staring into space. She'd lost her train of thought.

"Draw the line?" asked Max, peering into her eyes, searching for signs of life.

"Who the heck is *that?*" Summer Starlight Friedman asked nobody in particular, pointing over Max's shoulder.

Max turned around to see Molly Hannigan, ex-actress, ex-Sternberg wife, current Max Ramsey stalker, staring from twenty paces. She was holding an extra-large-head tennis racket at the ready like a gigantic fly swatter. She had on some kind of Victoria's Secret or Frederick's of Hollywood get-up. It was sexy, skimpy, and unbelievably pink. Hot pink doesn't come close. More like flaming day-glow pink...a surprising look for a coffee shop.

"Hi, Molly," said Max, "how are you?"

"Actually, Max, I've been better."

"Well," he replied, "at least you look good."

"Thank you, Max."

"So," he asked, "how did you even find me here?"

"I have my ways," she said, smacking her open palm with the racket, over and over, making a *ping, ping, ping* sound.

"Okay, fair enough," said Max, looking around at the

faces of the patrons and employees to gauge their level of nervousness. Okay, High Alert. Check.

Summer Starlight was frozen in her tracks, eyes wide, still holding the coffee pot. She looked remarkably like a freeze frame from *Happy Days*.

"So, Molly, you realize you're violating the restraining order, right?" He immediately knew this was a mistake, because the entire room gasped.

"Max," she replied, shaking her head, "passions do not always conform to the laws of men. Especially men like you."

"Okay, okay...got it. So why the tennis racket? It's no problem, just wondering, just asking questions here."

"I guess I just wanted to get everybody's attention."

"Yes, well, you did that," he said, looking around, nodding.

"You definitely have *my* attention," said Summer Starlight. "Hey, by the way. Are you Molly Hannigan? Because my parents are huge fans. Do you think I could get your autograph?"

Max sighed with relief. *Oh, my God. Thank you, Miss Summer Starlight Friedman.*

Molly smiled. "Well, sure. I'd be delighted."

The tension seemed to subside.

She walked over to the counter. "Calm down, Maxie. Can't you take a joke anymore?"

Summer Starlight handed Molly a menu and a pen. "Thank you so much. Their names are Joni and Garcia. That would be great. Wow. Yeah, I've never really seen you in a movie, but they are *so* into you."

Molly put down the racket, hunched over the counter, pen in air, and then hesitated. She seemed to be having some difficulty deciding where to sign and what to write. The menu had about a million items on it almost leaving no blank space at all. This was making Summer nervous. She kept talking.

"Yeah, so, anyway, one of these days I'm going to look up your old movies, because I'm really into vintage stuff, like clothes and stuff."

Molly closed her eyes. So did Max.

"Okay," said Molly, tapping the pen on the counter, "are you saying I'm *vintage?*"

"Oh, no," said Summer, "not at all. I mean, I think of vintage as a good thing, anyway, you know? But no, it's more like, you know, when you did your movies I wasn't even born yet, so I just don't know that much about them. You know, like, I know they're probably totally cool and everything, like *Gone with the Wind* and Laurel and Hardy, stuff like that, like classic Hollywood, you know?"

"Yeah," Molly said, "I know. I remind you of Laurel and Hardy."

Max jumped in. "I think what she's trying to say..."

But Summer interrupted.

"No, no, of course not, no, c'mon, you're nothing like Laurel and Hardy. I mean, they're crazy, funny guys in suits and funny hats and stuff, and, you know, they're *men*. So no, they're totally different. *Totally*. Jeez. I mean, they did black and white movies and you came in after color started, right? Wait, no. Were you in the black and white days? I mean I love the look of black and white. Vintage, like I said. No, I mean, you know, it's just that you're both, you know, *old*."

Molly glared at Summer, who realized what she'd done. She was afraid to even try to say anything to fix it. "I've said too much." She shut her eyes and gritted her teeth. Everyone in the room did the same. Everyone except Molly.

So she was literally the only person to fully see her perfectly executed forehand drive as it sliced through the pyramid of heavy, off-white, stone-wear coffee mugs, a multi-tiered mountain of cakes and croissants, and a couple of colorful point-of-purchase displays on the counter. Shards and shrapnel ricocheted everywhere, some actually becoming deeply embedded in the walls and ceiling. Her tennis swing had really come along. The pro at the club would have been very proud.

Somebody had called the police during the opening moments of this episode of the Molly Hannigan Reality Show. Three squad cars arrived, lights flashing, sirens screaming.

Molly snuck out the side door and disappeared into the mean streets of Brentwood, using the racket to machete her way through lush hedges that protect manicured backyards...terrifying old-money, new-money, and no-money undocumented gardeners and hipster coffee pourers alike.

Max ran after her. He had to help her if he could. He knew it could be the worst possible thing...she might think that his chasing her would mean that he wanted to be with her, that things might go back to the way they were. But he did care about her and he was worried something terrible might happen.

But by the time he reached the middle of Barrington Avenue——cars honking, drivers screaming——he'd lost sight of her.

"Molly! Come on, Molly! Come back, we need to talk."

Nothing. Max ran up the hill toward Brentwood Village, calling her name. One police car passed him, then another. But soon they circled back, obviously unable to find her. He tried her cell number, but it was out of service. He knew for a fact that they'd sold their house in the Palisades, so he couldn't even go there and wait for her.

He wondered if he should try to get in touch with her ex-husband or estranged daughter, but he knew they'd left town. Plus they both hated him. On the wild chance that he could actually track them down, he really could not see how getting a call out of the blue from their ex-wife-mom's despised ex-lover could possibly help anybody. He wasn't sure what to do next.

Chapter 27

Cynthia loved driving on empty freeways. It could not be more pleasurable. She had never before been to the Long Beach Yacht Club, but she did love the Long Beach Harbor... partly because of how unlike L.A. it was.

She had stayed at the Queen Mary Hotel a couple of times. It really gave you an idea of what travel used to be about. Glamor, leisure, social interaction...all the things you do not find at an airport today.

The harbor was also a huge, working city unto itself, blue collar, tons of people laboring hard instead of lying around pools making phone calls or waiting for the phone to ring.

The Yacht Club was on the beach, slightly separated from

the city. She pulled into the parking lot, noticing that the only non-luxury cars were pristine pick-up trucks used to tow smaller vessels.

She grabbed her suitcase and walked around to the docks, looking for Slip 225, the Radcliffe spot. She really knew nothing about sailing. She'd been a guest on a few boats, but they had been of the "sleeps-two" or "sleeps-none" variety. Walking along this network of docks, dwarfed by yacht after yacht, was like being a Lilliputian in a bathtub full of very, very expensive toy boats.

She found her way to Slip 225, where a thirteen year-old sailor was waiting next to a beautiful wooden motorboat. This was not the *boat*; this was the boat to *get* to the boat. They apparently had several of these kids ferrying guests over to the yacht, which was about two hundred yards offshore.

"Hi," said Sailor Boy, looking up from his *Mad Magazine*. "Are you part of the Radcliffe party? If so, you're too early."

"Yes, well, not exactly. I'm Cynthia Amas. I helped Ava put this whole thing together."

"Oh, right, yes," he said, standing up and dropping the *Mad* onto the chair, "Of course. Let's get you out there."

He assisted her down the ladder and started the engine.

It purred. This boat was gorgeous. The rich tones of

highly polished woods reminded Cynthia of a fine musical instrument--a Stradivarius or a Martin guitar. As a result, she thought of Pete, but she quickly turned to Sailor Boy, thinking that talking about something else would probably be a good thing.

"So is this what they call a Cigarette Boat?"

"Yes, that's a loose term, but yes. They call them Rum Runners too. Go-fast Boats. They have lots of nicknames. They used to use them to smuggle all kinds of stuff in the old days. In and out of Mexico, throughout the Great Lakes to Canada, stuff like that. I think Al Capone's guys used them to move booze in and out of Chicago and Wisconsin on Lake Michigan. Anyway, now they're the exclusive toys of the very rich. Mrs. Radcliffe has three and she only uses them to get out to the Que Sera Sarong. Most people just use crappy dinghies for that. These things go for more than a million each. Don't even ask what the big boat costs."

As he said that, he pointed ahead into the breeze. They were fast approaching a very large, very beautiful sailboat.

"Oh, I didn't realize Ava had money," said Cynthia.

This made the kid laugh.

They pulled up to the larger boat and Sailor Boy followed her up the ladder with her suitcase.

"What's your name, anyway?" she asked.

"Paul. Paul Winslow. That's my dad, Freddy, up there on the quarterdeck. He's the captain of this baby."

"Oh, wow," she said, "makes sense. Well, thanks for the ride."

"Adios!" he said disappearing behind the gunwale as he descended.

Cynthia could not believe how beautiful this yacht was. It felt like an impeccably designed art deco house. The fact that it was floating on the ocean made it that much more incredible.

Captain Winslow came down to greet her. He looked every bit as salty as he should be in his line of work. She half expected him to say, "I'm strongs to the finish, 'cause I eats me spinach."

"Cynthia," he said. "Welcome aboard."

"Thanks...glad to *be* aboard."

"I'm captain of the ship itself," he said, "but you're captain of everything else, as far as the eye can see."

"As far as the 'aye, aye' can see!" she said with a smile that said, "Sorry about that dumb nautical joke."

The captain rolled his eyes, but in a friendly way that said, "No problem, I've heard 'em all, lady."

He gave her a tour. There were lots of people scurrying around——crew members, the chef and *his* crew, and others. Her friend Will Grover had added very little in terms of decoration, mostly tasteful touches that almost seemed integral to the yacht's design——such as the dining room's table settings. The ballroom was adorned almost like a high school prom, except the materials were of the highest quality——instead of crepe paper, cascading curtains of black velvet; instead of a glittery disco ball...a huge Swarovski crystal ball. The place was amazing. It looked like Will could have spent thousands of dollars on it, but if she knew him, it was all on loan from one of the studios. He was a wiz at getting amazing free stuff.

They entered a large common room and there, in front of a gigantic fireplace, was the most massive bear rug she had ever seen.

She gasped when she saw it.

"Not to worry," said the captain. "I have it on good authority from your friend Will that it is 100% synthetic. I'm sure he's right. They don't grow bears that big."

Cynthia realized that was true. The rug was a whole lot bigger than a bear. And she was relieved. She knew for a fact that there were at least four vegetarians in the group.

She even wondered if some people would be freaked out by it anyway. But then she bent down and felt it. It was so soft and luxurious, she could totally imagine rolling around on it. Which was a good thing.

"Hey, Captain Freddy," she said. "Where's the nearest bathroom? Sorry. I mean, head."

"Right this way. Just around that screen. There are ten on board. But if I'm not mistaken, your bedroom is that one right over there. Obviously, there's a head in there too. Why don't you take your time, freshen up, and I'll see you around the deck."

"Shiver me timbers, Captain," she said.

"Hilarious, Captain," he replied.

Her bedroom was better than her bedroom at home. A lot better. She emptied the contents of her suitcase into the small built-in art deco dresser. She did that freshening up. She looked in the mirror and fixed her face. She wondered how she had gotten herself into this. The huge payday helped, of course, but she still wondered if this was the best thing for her business and her life.

She called her mother and got voicemail.

She called Pete and got the same.

She felt a little bit stranded. So much for the information

age. She was a problem solver by nature and by profession and she was feeling a bit too ineffectual for her taste.

Chapter 28

SATURDAY SOMETIME

The night before, when Max got back to the coffee shop, his briefcase and laptop were missing. Summer Starlight Friedman was gone. There was a new barista at the counter. A much more sullen coffee slinger...a bearded fellow with deep-set, heavy-lidded eyes and a permanent sneer.

"Hi," said Max. I was in here a while ago and I left my briefcase. There was a computer and a wallet in it."

"That was kind of stupid, wasn't it?" said the kid, measuring out espresso to make a cappuccino, "I mean, did you see the sign?"

The kid pointed to a sign on the wall, splattered with pastry, frosting, and bits of porcelain: "Do not leave items unattended. We are not responsible for them. So do not leave them. Ever. Got it? Good. -The Management"

"Okay," said Max, "but I'm not saying you're responsible, I'm just wondering if you could check in the lost and found or if anybody saw anybody suspicious."

"Listen, man," said Permanent Sneer Dude, "I know for a fact that there's nothing in the lost and found and aside from the crazy-ass lady who busted up the place before I came on shift, you are by far the most suspicious person here."

"Okay, great," said Max, "but could you possibly just check? It's important."

"Okay, man, I know there's nothing in there, but just a minute. I gotta finish this first."

He proceeded to steam milk for the cappuccino. It seemed like it took forever and then he just put the drink on the counter and got down on his knees and started rummaging through a bunch of stuff on a shelf.

Max looked at the cappuccino. "Don't you need to call someone for their coffee here? I mean somebody's waiting for that, right?"

Permanent Sneer Dude peered up over the edge of the counter. "That's for *me*, man."

Max resisted the impulse to strangle him.

Then the kid stood stood up, holding the briefcase. "This isn't it is it?"

"No, that *is* it," said Max, "See? Good you checked, right."

"Hey, I just found your lousy briefcase, man. I'd say a thank you is in order."

Max had had it.

"Didn't you see the sign?" he asked.

Permanent Sneer Dude looked around the room, then at Max. "Pff...what sign?"

"This sign," said Max, calmly giving him the finger.

"Hey, man, that is so not cool."

Max turned to leave, saying, "You're just lucky the crazy lady took her tennis racket with her."

He thought he would drive around the neighborhood looking for Molly, but when he got to the spot where he'd parked his car, it was gone. He ran up and down the block... did he forget where he parked it? No. Not only couldn't he look around for Molly, he had no way to get down to Long Beach.

"Jesus Christ, what next?!" he cried.

"What happened?" said a female voice in the dark.

Max looked over only to see the orange glow of a cigarette.

"Molly?"

"Nope, Summer."

"Summer?"

"Yeah, Summer Starlight Friedman."

"Oh, Summer! The girl who just could not stop insulting Molly Hannigan...calling her old and saying she looked like Laurel or Hardy or vintage cheese or something ... were you *trying* to make her snap?"

"I know," she said, starting to cry. "Sometimes when I'm nervous, I just blab. And I cannot stop blabbing. I'm an idiot." She was starting to sob.

"No, no, no," said Max. "It wasn't your fault. Molly has a lot of problems. She just went through a divorce; her daughter's not speaking to her. Her daughter *left the country* to get away from her. She's a mess. It's partly my fault too. I was...well, never mind. Anyway, it's not your fault."

"Well, yeah," she said. "But there's something else. After she ran out and you chased after her and the cops came and then they left...it was really crazy, there was broken glass and food everywhere. Some people were crying, they were pretty freaked out. But then, she came back."

"Who?" asked Max. "Molly?"

"Yeah, it was weird. I mean, obviously it was weird, but she walked up to the counter. I didn't even realize that the cops were gone until I saw her and realized she must have waited until they left."

"Well, what happened?"

"Yeah, so, she came up to the counter carrying a briefcase. She said it was yours and that she came back because she'd noticed it there on the table and didn't want it to get stolen. So, you know, she brought it to me."

"Wow, that was sort of nice of her, I guess. I mean, she's a good person...just a bit, you know, confused."

"Yeah," said Summer, "but then when I took the briefcase, she did something kinda weird. I mean, it was all weird, but this was...well, she held up some keys and shook them and laughed. And then she ran out."

Max was putting it together. "Wait, you mean..." He did a quick check of his case: yup, keyless.

"At the time," Summer said, starting to cry again, "I thought she was just shaking her own keys as just another weird, crazy thing to do. I had no idea she'd gotten them out of your case until I saw you realizing that your car was gone. I am sooo sorry. I'm an idiot."

"No, no," he said. "Stop saying that. You're not an idiot. How could you know those were my keys? But I do have a favor to ask."

"Anything. You name it."

"Well, it is a big favor."

"Oh, well, wait, what is it. Maybe I spoke too soon about the anything thing."

"Give me a ride to Long Beach?"

"Long Beach?"

"I know. It's a long way, but..."

"Long Beach? I *live* in Long Beach. But, wait, what about your car? Don't you need to call the cops or something."

"Nah," said Max. "It's a rental."

"Okay," said Summer Starlight Friedman, "our chariot awaits."

The chariot was a 1964 Ford Falcon station wagon, covered with graffiti.

"Wow," said Max, "somebody tagged you good."

"What, that? *I* did that. I'm an artist. Duh." She opened the passenger side and gathered up a pile of sketchbooks, art supplies, small canvasses, and heaved them over onto a much larger mountain of the same stuff in the backseat. Then she removed a parking ticket from under the windshield wiper, crumpled it, and threw it back there too.

They got in.

"I love your archival storage system," he said, smiling. He was beginning to like her.

"Shut up, crazy lady stalk-ee. Okay, listen," she continued. "I don't know about you——well, actually I kinda do know about you——but I've had a long day. I need a drink. There's a bottle in the glove compartment. And, no, I am not going to drink and drive. I'm going to drink a little bit and *then* drive. Then you can drink *while* I drive."

"That is the best idea I've heard all day," he said, finding the bottle of bourbon and twisting the cap.

She took a rather large gulp, more like she was drinking water than whisky. She stared at the bottle for a moment and then took an even bigger chug. She sighed deeply and started the car.

"Hold on, Summer, are you okay to drive?"

"I have been drinking coffee for eight hours straight. What do *you* think?"

"I think I'm driving."

"What? No way."

"Yes way. Get over here."

They switched places...he, under...she, over.

"Okay, let's agitate the gravel, baby," he said.

"Wow, cool, daddy-o," she said, taking another swig. "You

speak my language."

Max pulled out onto San Vicente, left on Wilshire, on the way to the 405.

"Hey," he said, "back before the craziness started, you said you didn't smoke. And then, back there on the sidewalk..."

"Yeah, well, I had quit. But your girlfriend back there..."

"She is not my girlfriend."

"Okay, let me rephrase: your batshit crazy cuckoo bird *ex*-girlfriend knocked me off the smoking *and* drinking wagon."

"Really? So when did you quit?" He hit the freeway ramp and accelerated into the flow of traffic, if you can call what a forty-year-old Falcon does accelerating.

"Last night I quit drinking. Today, before I went on shift I quit smoking. Hey, now I got a question for *you*. What the hell is your name?"

Max couldn't believe how adorable and charming Summer was turning out to be. She was actually quite beautiful in a messy art-girl way. He was also amazed that he had absolutely no interest in making any kind of move on her. He felt protective of her. It felt like she could be his daughter. This was a brand new feeling for him. He had never wanted to have kids. He had never even really felt paternal toward anyone.

As they rode along and talked, he enjoyed the feeling.

"My name is Max," he said. "Max Ramsey."

Summer burst out laughing, hitting the dashboard with the palm of her hand. "What, is *everyone* named Max?"

"What? What are you talking about?"

"My boyfriend is Max. Oh, and by the way, we need to pick him up, but it's right on the way."

"Summer, we're kind of in a hurry here."

"Yeah, well, I don't really care," she said. "You can walk if you want to."

"Okay, where am I going?"

"Venice. He's a tattoo artist at the beach."

"Good God, no," said Max and as he said it he felt oddly fatherly again.

"Oh," she said, "so you don't approve, Daddy-o? Well at least he's not a crazy stalker like some people's significant others I know."

"She is not my significant other."

"Okay, whatever. So how do you happen to know Steven Sternberg's wife, anyway?"

"Ex-wife. Long story."

She scrunched down in the seat with the bottle. "Hey, we've got time."

Chapter 29

By the time she emerged from her cabin, many guests were arriving. She looked out over the rail to see two of the cigarette boats heading toward her and one heading back.

She wondered if Paloma had arrived yet. Her phone plinked. An email from Ava.

Cynthia-

Thank you so much for coming to the opening. It was a rousing success. I wanted to pass the name on to you that I mentioned. He's an old friend of Jonathon's. And me too. A very entertaining fellow and single again. His name is Max Ramsey. And he will be joining us.

See you soon,

ADR

Somehow Cynthia was not surprised. Amused and horrified, but not surprised. Max seemed to know just about everyone in the world. It was problematic to say the least, that there was so much history between him and Lolita and her and, as it turns out, Ava, even if they were just friends. The concept of this whole weekend was getting more muddled by the minute.

"Cynthia, it's so good to see you." Cynthia looked up to see Ava Dodd Radcliffe in the flesh, as if she simply materialized from the email. "Have you found your bedroom? Is everything satisfactory?"

"Everything is wonderful," said Cynthia. "I have a rough itinerary here, but I really think you mostly want these two days to be as spontaneous as possible."

"Oh, I agree. In fact, other than meals and general gatherings, I think it would be much better to stay away from formal activities, don't you think?"

"Definitely." Cynthia was beginning to wonder why she needed to be there. Nonetheless, she was kind of happy to be there--especially relatively free of responsibilities.

"So, you got the email about my friend Max?"

"Yes," said Cynthia. And then she said something that she

immediately regretted. "I look forward to meeting him." She didn't really know exactly why she lied, pretending that she didn't know him, but she did. The whole thing was getting a bit out of control. Ava knew Jack and Max. What did it matter that she knew Max? What was the point of lying? To just not have to explain it all, she supposed.

"Yes, well," said Ava, "I've told him about you and he is looking forward to meeting you as well. As for me," she continued, heading for the ladder, "I'd better go greet some guests."

Cynthia was relieved that she wasn't caught in a lie, but also nervous that the lie that Max had conveniently corroborated would be exposed later. Just thinking about Jack Stone and Max being on the same boat together was beyond horrifying.

Cynthia took out her phone to remind herself of the list of the eleven "complicateds" who had confirmed:

Ivana Corbin, mathematician and singer

Mary Lou Fetzer, jewelry designer

Gloria Bunk, local talk show host

Tia Barlow, special counsel to the mayor of San Diego

Rosa Marianza, vegan chef and cookbook author

Charlotte Nordine, ex-dancer and choreographer

Philip Corso, graffiti artist-turned fashion mogul

Timothy Brion, musician

Mikal Zedonia, surfer, cellist with the Santa Barbara Symphony

Roger Edson, entrepreneur

Zed MacMurtry, gentleman cowboy

Seamus O'Brien, aspiring writer, charmer, ex-cab driver

Plus Ava, Jack Stone, and Max, makes fifteen participants.

Plus Paloma and herself...supposedly working, but Cynthia was starting to have the sneaking suspicion that there wouldn't really be a lot of work to do. She knew every single person on the boat, except for some of the crew. What was she going to do, sit in her bedroom or wander around, pretending to be invisible? At this point, the weekend was a certainly messy, potentially disastrous melting pot of personalities. She knew she had neither the authority nor the capability of controlling what happened. In some ways it was a grand experiment. It was up to each participant to make of it what they may.

And may god have mercy on their souls, she thought to herself, and then laughed out loud.

"What's so funny?" asked Paloma, who Cynthia had not seen arriving by boat, and was suddenly standing before her.

"Oh, life, I guess," said Cynthia, smiling. "I just hope everyone makes it back alive."

"It is kind of exciting," said Paloma, watching a young dark-skinned stud coming aboard. He was wearing only long, surfer-style, paisley patterned swim trunks ... no shirt and no shoes. He was seriously built and carrying a small duffle bag, so apparently there wasn't a whole lot he was planning on changing into. He had an electric smile that immediately charmed all humans, female and male, within a hundred-yard radius. It was like a charm pirate had just commandeered the ship and was set to plunder and pillage any and all of the available booty aboard.

"That's Mikal," said Cynthia.

"Zedonia," said Paloma.

"Yeah," sighed Cynthia, "breathtaking. When I met him, he was, you know, clothed."

Paloma smiled. "I suggest we stack a deck of cards and challenge him to one hand of strip poker."

Cynthia laughed out loud.

"What's so funny?" asked a woman from behind her.

"That seems to be the question on everybody's lips," said

Cynthia, turning around to see Lolita in her blue and white yacht-club-stripper attire. "Jesus," she said. "You are certainly dressed for success."

Paloma giggled, but Lolita did not.

"I think it's very tasteful," she said.

"And tasty," said Cynthia. "But seriously, you look beautiful."

"Oh, thanks," replied Lolita.

Pretty soon the yacht was filling up. There was an amazing spread of food in the dining room and conversation was lively. For Cynthia, especially, it was like old home week, because she had met every single person and knew intimate details about them all. So far, no Max and no Jack.

She looked across the room and saw Paloma talking with Seamus. They made an adorable couple and now she was feeling a little sorry for him, since Paloma had said she wasn't really interested.

There was a crowd around Ava, who was looking as lovely as ever. She was the only one who didn't look a bit out of place. Her clothing seemed to be provided by the boat's designer: sleek, classy, and sexy.

Timothy Brion, the musician, approached Cynthia.

"Hi. Nice to see you again."

"Hi, Tim, I'm so glad you could come."

"Oh, wouldn't miss it. I know I must be a bit of a hard case, in terms of matchmaking. Musicians tend to be avoided like the plague by civilians."

"Yeah, well, no, don't think that way, you know, there are lots of..." she started to answer, trying to look on the bright side for him. But then she simply gave up. "Oh, who am I trying to kid. You're right. A girl would need to be half crazy to look for a long-term, lasting relationship with someone who is on the road two hundred and fifty days a year."

Timothy was a little taken aback. After all, Cynthia had been incredibly optimistic and supportive when they'd met. She had all kinds of ideas for dates for him, but then she'd sort of dropped it. And now she was so disarmingly honest. At first he felt a little angry, but then an appreciation of her straight-forwardness set in.

"I can't say I expected that, but I do find it refreshingly blunt."

"Oh, Tim, I'm sorry. I'm just going through my own thing with a musician right now and it's probably coloring my view a bit."

"On tour?"

"Big time. Long time. Seems like forever actually."

"Yeah," said Timothy. "Can I get you another glass of wine?"

"Do they have anything stronger?"

"Cynthia Amas, now you are talking."

He headed for the bar.

Cynthia surveyed the scene. People were taking their meals and spreading out, heading down the deck, paired off into small groups. She wondered where Jack was. And Max. Not that surprising really, they were both late types. She was a bit anxious because the entire event seemed so fraught with potential misunderstanding and jealousy. She wasn't completely sure about Ava's stability to begin with.

Just as she stepped in their direction, Timothy returned with two very large margaritas.

"Oh my God, that looks good," she said.

They toasted musicians and musician lovers everywhere. Timothy was really a very charming guy. He had the kind of face that reminded you of him when he was a kid, even though you didn't *know* him as a kid.

They clinked glasses.

"Does this whole trip remind you of *Titanic* just a little bit?" he asked.

"More than a little bit," she replied. "I doubt the ship will sink, but a few hearts might."

"What are the other movies about boats?" he asked. "I was thinking about *The Cat's Meow,* have you seen that one?"

"No, I don't think so. Maybe part of it on TV. It's the one about Chaplin and a murder, right?"

"Right, well it's Kirsten Dunst as Marion Davies, William Randolph Hearst's mistress, you know. Bogdanovich directed it. They go out with a bunch of famous movie people... Chaplin is played by what's his name, the comedian in the dress...Eddie Izzard, and I can't remember who plays Thomas Ince, Louella Parsons, and they others. It's Ince's birthday. But anyway, Hearst is a jealous man...understandable, he's sort of a big, fat, old man having this long-term affair with a beautiful starlet...I mean, the Hearst Castle, the Santa Monica beach house, all of that was for her. And he suspects Chaplin is screwing her. And he probably is...I mean, he's Charlie Fucking Chaplin, right? And Ince is kind of fueling the fires of Hearst's jealousy, snooping around, digging up evidence, and at one point, Ince tries on Chaplin's derby and Hearst mistakes him for Chaplin and——pow——he shoots him. Dead. Then they all take a secrecy pact. The End."

"Wow," said Cynthia. "Well, yeah. That could totally happen here."

Timothy laughed very hard and so did Cynthia, but she was actually a little worried that something like that could happen this weekend. Not murder. Something less violent, but equally weird.

They got two more margaritas and just as Cynthia swallowed her first sip, Timothy leaned in and kissed her full on the mouth.

"Oh, my," she said, "that tasted good."

Chapter 30

SATURDAY EVENING

It was almost eight o'clock when Jack Stone pulled into the parking lot of the Long Beach Yacht Club. He had been there many times before and, in fact, had a boat of his own——a gorgeous racing catamaran, a very fast double-hulled sailboat——moored there for years. For a while, he'd been fairly heavily involved in Formula-18 Catamaran competition. He was an excellent skipper and he absolutely loved it——he'd won some races——but finding the time was almost impossible since he'd become an international film star committed to making one, sometimes two, sometimes three films a year. He realized a few years back that he'd either have to give up sailing or "romancing" and, well, that was that.

He cut through the clubhouse, thinking he'd just say a quick hello to the salty old dogs he'd gotten to know over the years. They were pretty much always there.

He entered the bar and immediately a few patrons called out, "Jack!" "Where've ya been, ya lousy land lubber!" and "That last movie, *The Long Way Down*, sure was a sorry piece of flotsam and jetsam! You shoulda been sailing!"

"Ha, ha! Very funny," he said throwing his arms around two of the ancient mariners who seemed like they hadn't moved from those very stools since the last time he'd seen them. "Do you two ever go home?"

"What? We *are* home," said one.

"We have our priorities straight," said another, "unlike some Hollywood pussies we know."

This got a laugh from all corners of the room.

"Jack, me boy," said another, "I want you to meet some new friends of mine. This is Summer and her boyfriend, Max. We call him Tatted Max, to avoid confusion."

Summer and her boyfriend, who was covered with tattoos on every square inch of visible skin except portions of his face, turned around.

"Wow," said Tatted Max, "Jack Fucking Stone."

"Hi, nice to meet you," said Jack, reaching out to shake his hand.

Summer, teetering from the alcohol, intercepted Jack's hand and shook it enthusiastically while smiling her sweetest possible smile. "So," she said, "one of the douches who screwed up Molly Hannigan."

During the car ride, Max had related the entire sordid tale to Summer and Tatted Max about how he and Jack had been involved in a wild fracas at the palatial estate of Sternberg and Hannigan, who Jack and Max had both been screwing on the side. Since Tatted Max had taken over the driving when he hopped aboard at Venice Beach, Max was able to imbibe in the bourbon, thereby sliding comfortably into the mood for revealing secrets.

Max told them that at the time, he had been unperturbed by it all. In fact, that day had ended happily for him...he'd ridden off with the lovely Lolita on her cute, tight, pink Vespa, both literally, and then, later, literally did exactly what that sounds like metaphorically. They'd had a really good time for seventy-seven hours straight...with occasional breaks for other forms of sustenance. He remembered seventy-seven because they'd gotten a hotel on the Sunset Strip and, noticing the time as they were finally packing up, started singing the old TV theme song. Above all, he wanted fun——and for him sex was fun's major ingredient——every single day of his life. He said he'd often lied to others in the pursuit of this happiness, but that he never lied to himself. Today's events had given him pause. Not just seeing Molly again, but also spending time with Summer. For the first time in years he found himself at least wanting to try to tell fewer lies. He was really looking forward to seeing Lolita.

Jack, on the other hand, had always been more deluded. Fifty percent of his lies were ones he told himself. He somehow believed he *wasn't* lying. He was in a continual state of self-deception.

Summer and Jack were still shaking hands, but the shaking slowed, and then stopped. Jack was understandably stunned by what she'd said. "What? Wait, who are you again?"

One of the old guys said, "Never mind, Jack. I want you to meet the *other* Max. This guy's a hoot and a half."

Max Ramsey slowly twirled around in his chair. Of course, he knew exactly whom he was going to see, but Jack did not have the same advantage.

Max held out his hand.

"Hi, Jack, I'm Max."

"A pleasure to..." Jack reached out his hand, but then

stopped. "Wait...I know you, right?"

Max could not resist. He could never resist a joke.

"Well," he said, "we know some of the same *women*, although from what I hear, I know them a *whole lot better*."

"Oh, right!" he gasped. "You're Cynthia's *brother*! From Fiji! You sick motherfucker, or should I say *sister*-fucker!"

This only made Max laugh. He had pretended that Cynthia was his sister, but after all the revelations that had flown by, Stone still had never caught on that it was just a joke. He could not stop laughing. Summer and Tatted Max were also laughing because in the car Max had shared the sister-fucking story: "And I bet you a gazillion bucks that Jack Stone still hasn't figured it out."

Summer turned to Tatted Max: "We owe Untatted Max a gazillion dollars." This made the three of them laugh even harder.

Which made Jack even madder.

"What the hell are you lunatics laughing about?" He hated Max for two main reasons: One, the sister incest thing. For no good or logical reason, he did not hold Cynthia responsible whatsoever for complicity in this imagined incest. And two, he hated Max because, even though Max had caused just as much tumult and heartache as he did during the Sternberg incident, while Jack lost three movies, his best friend, several lovers in a dwindling stable, the respect of many of his peers and fans, and a large chunk of his leg to a mad Chihuahua——well, not mad, but definitely very angry——Max had escaped unscathed. He had beat Jack at his own game.

Max didn't hate Jack. He just thought he was an asshole and an idiot. Period. And he loved shining a light on his asshole-ness and idiocy. He found it entertaining.

The patrons of the yacht club bar were confused. The two attitudes——smoldering rage versus giddy amusement——seemed odd, to say the least.

Of course, Max refused to explain. He loved that Jack was shocked and enraged for all the wrong reasons.

"To get back to your point," he said, "yes, I came all the way from Fiji to rendezvous with my baby sister out on Ava Dodd Radcliffe's little dinghy."

"You are not going out on that yacht!" said Jack, sounding righteous and noble in the defense of sisterhood and womankind, and everything, really.

"OH. I'M SORRY," Max said in a much too loud voice. "ARE YOU DEAF? BECAUSE I JUST SAID THAT'S WHERE I AM GOING. MY SISTER IS EXPECTING ME. SHE HAS A THING FOR THE GENTLE ROCKING OF

THE SEA. SHE'D PROBABLY LOVE TRAINS FOR THE SAME REASON. MENTAL NOTE: BOOK TRAIN RIDE WITH SIS."

Summer, Tatted Max, and the bar patrons were amused, entranced, disgusted, or a combination of those things.

"You sick wannabe," said Jack, fuming...breathing heavier now.

"YEAH," said Max with a shrug. "YOU SIMPLY CANNOT BEAT SOME LITTLE SISTER LOVIN'."

That was it. Jack lunged forward, swinging hard, but Max knew it was coming...he'd intentionally driven him to do it. He quickly grabbed a nearby chair, lion tamer style, and Jack slammed his fist into one of the metal legs.

"Oww! You asshole!" he screamed, still coming.

Summer wanted to get into the fight, but Tatted Max held her back, while Max picked up a nearby pint of ale and rocketed the contents into Jack's face.

This slowed him down, but not by much.

Max threw the empty glass at him...and sprinted for the door, the two kids right behind him. They dragged one of the round tables with them, lodged it in the open doorway, and headed for the dock.

Jack tripped over at least three chairs before struggling

with the obstruction in the doorway.

The odd trio made it to Slip 225.

"Hello, Mr. Ramsey," said Paul Winslow, who happened to be carefully folding the last page of his *Mad Magazine*, the *Mad* Fold-In. "What's the hurry?"

Max had been aboard Ava and Jonathon's boat many times. He really was just a friend to Ava. "Get me to Ms. Radcliffe's boat, Paul. Pronto," he said, leaping into the cigarette boat, Summer and Tatted Max right behind him. "There's a crazy movie star in there who's off his meds. And he's taking it out on me. Us."

"Sure thing, Max." Paul moved fast. "You're lucky, I'm the last guy here and I was about to go home. The yacht already sailed, but we can catch it."

He cast off, powered up, and by the time Jack reached the end of the dock, they were already thirty yards out.

"Good man, Paul. This is Summer and Tatted Max. You know, when I was a kid I was the only Max around. There were probably five Maxes under seventy years old in the country. Now the planet is lousy with Maxes."

"Hey, who are you calling lousy?" asked Tatted Max.

"I'm just saying that the nation has sort of maxed out on Maxes, that's all."

"There are definitely twice as many Maxes on this boat than there should be," said Summer, giving Max Ramsey a fake evil eye.

"Well," said Paul, "friends of this Max are friends of mine." Then, squinting toward shore, "Hey, isn't that Jack Stone?"

"Yes," said Max. "Poor fellow. As much of an asshole-creep as he is, you gotta feel for those tormented by the scourge of mental illness."

"I had no idea. I used to see him around here all the time. And I can testify to the fact that he was a total asshole to me. I guess that was why."

"No," said Summer, "he's an asshole even when he's sane."

Meanwhile, the dock was crowded with angry, drunken denizens of the bar, all shaking their fists and trying hard to outdo one another with loud, colorful, nautical expletives. Jack was their man. Their man in Hollywood, goddamn it. They had only met Max and the others a half an hour ago. Plus, they didn't take kindly to incest.

Paul looked back, squinting at the dock again. It was dark and visibility was low.

"So...I guess *all* those old dudes are off their meds?"

They all burst into laughter and were still laughing when

they finally reached the Que Sera Sarong. Max, Tatted Max, and Summer climbed the ladder.

"Thanks, matey," Max said. "I tell you what. If you can delay Jack from getting over here, there's something in it for you. And if the deal I'm working on hits, the something will be a number with a lot of zeros."

"Avast!" Paul called over the sound of the motor, "We pirates have to stick together!"

Chapter 31

Max and company wandered into the dining room where a whole new spread of food and drink had been laid out. Loud party music was playing too, but except for two couples dancing and a couple of the chef's assistants, the place was empty. The party had apparently spread to all corners of the yacht. They loaded up plates with all kinds of gourmet offerings and then poured champagne.

Max had no doubt that Jack would be coming for him. But since he would need to hitch a ride with Paul (who would happily do anything he could to delay his least-favorite asshole even without his offer of monetary gain) or one of the bar relics (who would need a lot of coaxing and black coffee to abandon their boat-style bar stools for an actual boat, even for Jack), and the wind had picked up, so the yacht was now pointing, moving along at a very fast clip, they'd have time to relax a bit.

They ate and drank, gazing at the star-filled sky with the wind in their faces. They watched the lights of North America fade and disappear over the watery horizon.

"This may be the most beautiful place on Earth," said Summer, putting her arm around Tatted Max.

Max refreshed their champagne glasses and headed over to the rail. He could see several boats, their headlights dancing like fireflies along the surface of the sea. One of those sets of lights might be Jack coming for some kind of macho showdown.

"Hey, you guys," he said. "I'm going to go look for some people. They've gotta be here somewhere." He walked along the deck, wondering where everyone was. He wanted to see Ava, just because she was a very good friend and he wanted to check in on how she was doing. He felt protective of her after Jonathon passed away. He wanted to see Cynthia; just to say that he got it, that he knew it was over. He wanted to see Lolita for other reasons.

He walked along, coming across various couples and small

parties of guests chatting and drinking. The acoustics were peculiar since the sound of the wind and waves gave all of these sequestered groups their own auditory sense of privacy. Their conversations and laughter could not be heard until Max was right up close to them and then immediately dissipated as he passed, swallowed up by the great white noise of the sea.

He made a complete lap of the deck and still couldn't find anybody he knew. He passed Summer and Tatted Max, who had curled up in a hammock and were either asleep or just in some kind of meditative state of communal bliss. He thought they looked adorable. Even though he knew no one was seeking, nor cared to hear it, he found himself approving of Tatted Max.

Max continued his search, but this was weird...sort of a largely invisible party. He put his ear to one cabin door, then another, hoping to hear something that would provide a clue. But the wind in his ears, the luffing of the sails, and the rush of water against the hull was far too loud.

Then he heard the putt-putt-putting of a motorboat slowing down, then silence, and he knew it was time to make a decision.

He tried one doorknob. Locked. He hadn't thought about

that. The next one: locked. He heard the motorboat rev again. Jack had to be climbing the ladder at this point.

Max tried the next, the next, the next: locked, locked, locked. Finally one turned. He pushed the door open quickly and quietly and locked it behind him.

It was pitch dark in there. He might have heard breathing... he wasn't sure. It could have been the wind. He just stood there. He couldn't turn on a light, which might attract the attention of the rabid movie star who was undoubtedly patrolling the perimeter right now, looking for any excuse to bust down any door.

He opted for standing still as a statue for a while, there in the dark. He didn't know how long. He was playing this by ear. He kept thinking he could hear something close by, but he wasn't sure. And he was reluctant to even whisper a hello, because that could lead to a scream, which could lead to lights, and god knew what else.

One thing about Max was that he was able to laugh at himself in even the direst circumstances. He started to chuckle softly. He couldn't help it. He tried to hold it in, but it could not be denied. He covered his mouth with his hands, which led to soft *sniff-sniff-sniff-type* laughter through his nose.

Then, from the darkness, came a voice, a sweet woman's voice, saying, "Hello? Is there somebody in here?"

Chapter 32

Cynthia had been in her room with Timothy for a long time.

She had said, "Timothy, would you mind just talking for a while?"

He had said, "I'd love that."

What was it about musicians? How ridiculous could she get, she wondered. Her long-distance relationship with Pete was falling apart and here she was sitting on a bed on the verge of falling into it with another one.

She was attracted to him. He had the kind of strong, but soft voice that she found intoxicating. He wasn't forcing himself on her at all, but she was slowly being drawn in.

He was in the middle of a sentence. He was talking to her about why he loved re-reading Raymond Chandler since he moved to Los Angeles. He had lived here for a couple of years before he'd spent any real time downtown. And just a few months ago, he'd bought a loft in a converted old office building on Broadway smack in the middle of downtown. Its ceilings were twenty feet high and he was on the twenty-seventh floor. The view was glorious, she really needed to come over and check it out. He was also an artist, not professionally, but he had actually gone to art school. In his spare time he built things. The first thing he made when he moved into his loft space was a huge sculpture of a couple...embracing, kissing, floating high up near the ceiling. They were twenty feet long, their legs and arms entwined, weightless, like the figures in a Chagall painting. They were covered with words, collaged typography, some readable, some overlapping, fragments left to the viewer to finish and interpret. He had a picture of it on his iPhone and it was gorgeous and sexy and a monumental testament to love and life. And the thing that Cynthia liked most about it was that he wasn't doing it for money or fame or anything else. He was a successful musician...he had no intention or desire to switch over to making art.

"I made this piece to please only myself. I tried to make my own thoughts on love and relationships and human bondage manifest, custom-made for this spectacular living space overlooking a downtown that is an unrecovered time capsule of another age. And my neighbors and I are trying to help drag it into the 21st century."

Cynthia liked him. He reminded her of Pete. But when it came down to it, she liked Pete more. Plus, she kept thinking about Ava. Where was she? Was she mingling? Was this entire enterprise a total bust? She wasn't here for herself. And somehow, weirdly, she could see Timothy and Ava together.

"Timothy," she said, "have you met Ava yet?"

"No, not really. I saw her across the deck earlier."

"Because," she said, "I don't know...I think maybe you should."

"But I thought I was in the middle of meeting *you*," said Timothy.

"Yeah, well, yes, that's true, you were. I like you and I'm flattered. But I've already got one musician. I think I do anyway. In any case, I'm not in the market for another one at the moment."

She called Ava.

"Cynthia?"

"Yup. What's going on with you?"

"I'm with an old friend and a new friend. Just talking. About you."

"Oh, God, don't tell me. Max and who else? Oh, Ava, I'm so sorry...I should have told you that I know him. And warned you about him. I also have a history with Jack. I'm so embarrassed at how incestuous this night has become. I don't know what to say."

"Don't say anything. Max is just a friend. And we're only saying good things about you. Lolita's here too."

"Oh. Well. Good. I guess?"

"Yeah," said Ava. "It is good. She's marvelous. I do wish I could have met someone tonight, but I'm in a good place. Maybe next time. I'm getting the distinct feeling that these two are wanting some alone time."

"Oh, yeah," said Cynthia, "they do seem to be craving alone time a lot lately. But listen, I do have someone I'd like you to meet." Cynthia was getting the tingling feeling she got when her intuition was firing on all cylinders. "I've got a good feeling about this. I think you should come to my cabin."

She looked at Timothy. "This might be crazy, but I like you

both so much."

"I don't know," he said, "I'm no billionaire."

"Yeah, I know, but that might be a good thing. See you later."

She stepped out onto the deck. The cold breeze hit her face. It was invigorating. She hadn't felt at all sleepy before, but suddenly she was a hundred times more awake. She climbed the stairs to the quarterdeck, looking for someone. She found him.

"Ahoy, Captain," she said.

"Ditto, Captain," said Captain Winslow.

Chapter 33

Ava knocked on the door and it opened. "I'm Timothy," he said.

"I'm Ava."

"I know. Hi. Come in. Okay, this is awkward. Welcome to your yacht. I'm pretending to be hospitable when you're the only generous host around here. Do you want a drink or something? I know I do. "

Ava smiled. She liked him already. "To tell you the truth, I'm starving. I haven't eaten anything all night. Such a weird night, you know? Are you hungry at all?"

"I'm always hungry," he said.

"Good," she replied, calling Sutherland on speed dial. "I love hungry people. And thirsty people. Sutherland, hi, can you bring us something? Surprise us. Something light. But good. And two of everything. Oh, Sutherland, you know me too well. Yes, champagne, please, yes, obviously. Thanks."

"So," said Ava, "tell me about yourself."

Chapter 34

Jack was still stalking his prey. He, unlike Max, had been less hesitant about barging in on people and knocking on locked doors. The way in which he was received was, again, a stunning demonstration of the special treatment accorded the rich and famous.

He walked in on Charlotte Nordine, the thirty-year-old ex-ballet dancer and choreographer, while she was rather energetically making love to Philip Corso, the graffiti artist-turned fashion mogul. He was wearing only cowboy boots. She, only a yellow balloon animal of indeterminate species adorning her head like a crown in some kind of X-rated kingdom on a sick and twisted kid's show.

When the door flew open she whipped her head around in fear to see who was intruding, but when she saw who it was, she smiled.

"If I'm having a dream," she said, "don't wake me."

Philip was similarly undeterred. "I. Have. A. Script," he said, pumping slowly, rhythmically. "I'd. Like. You. To. Read."

"Not tonight," said Jack, walking in, and checking the bathroom and under the bed with the precision of a military man. "Okay, well, I'm looking for someone, so I've gotta get going," said Jack, heading for the door.

"Well. Don't. Be. A. Stranger," said Carlotta, the word "stranger" morphing into a cat-like howl.

The next door was locked, so Jack just pounded on it without a split second of hesitation. This was an *emergency*. In fact, while he was pounding he said, "Open up, this is an unbelieveable emergency!"

Mikal Zedonia, super-hunk surfer and cellist, came to the door with a panicked look in his eye and a full erection. He was wearing a black lace bra, but backwards.

"What, did we hit an iceberg or something? Are we going down?" Which was ironic because he had been going down on the beautiful young redhead, Tia Barlow, the special counsel to the mayor of San Diego.

She crawled out from under the blanket.

"No," said Jack, scanning the room, "Someone's gone missing... I'm looking for him. Guy named Max. I'm, you know, worried about him. Have you seen him?"

"Max was here a while ago," said Tia, "but he left. He was looking for someone too."

Jack's anger rose and he finished his search quickly before heading out.

"Wait," said Tia, grabbing a Que Sera Sarong pen and paper. "Could I have your autograph? I loved you in *The Long Way Down*."

This stopped Jack in his tracks. Nobody liked that movie. "You loved me in *The Long Way Down*? I directed that too, you know."

"Oh, I know," she said, "I have it on Blu-ray. I've watched it like fifty times."

"Really," said Jack, signing the piece of paper. "Maybe I could get *your* name and number?"

Tia giggled and obliged, but Mikal got up, grabbed the paper and crumpled it up, so Jack left empty handed.

He moved farther along the deck and put his ear to another door. He heard something. He tried the doorknob. It opened.

There was Lolita, sitting up in bed, watching a George Clooney movie on TV, a mountain of covers pulled up around her...only her head and lovely bare shoulders visible. The comforter was undulating slightly. It was obvious to Jack Stone that she was pleasuring herself to George Clooney. Jack Stone hated George Clooney. Something about a stolen girlfriend, a lost movie role, and overall career envy. Lolita had heard about it from Cynthia.

"Jack!" she said with a huge smile, pulling out one hand to wave. The comforter continued to move rhythmically.

"Hi," he said, looking away, then looking back. "So, how...how...have you..." Jack seemed to recognize Lolita, but clearly had no idea why. "...how have you, you know, been?" Even though Lolita was indirectly responsible for Jack getting involved with Second Acts and subsequently Cynthia, technically they had never met. His dog, Scarlett O'Hara, had fraternized with her dogs at the shop...one thing led to another, word of mouth, etc., etc., and Jack ended up contacting Cynthia, and the rest is history. Or at least hysteria. Lolita had also witnessed Jack in all his massive dick-swinging glory at the Sternberg party, when, not all but certainly quite a few of his toxic chickens came home to roost and proceeded to lay an avalanche of rotten-egg life lessons upon him, which he seemed to have learned absolutely nothing from. And to top it off, of course, her dog Wilfredo had made a meal out of his right thigh, which was incredibly entertaining for everyone except him. But she had no idea if he'd even noticed her. She didn't take it personally. Hard to concentrate on girl watching when you're naked and gushing blood in front of dozens of stunned guests. But that didn't mean she couldn't have fun with him now.

"Oh, you know, same old, same old," she said. "Nothing really new since last we...well, you know...*met*." It was the dirtiest pronunciation of the word "met" that Jack had ever heard. Max appreciated it too and he was having trouble containing his laughter under the covers, which were moving a little faster now.

"Okay..." Jack said nervously, eyes darting around the room, simultaneously trying to remember how he knew her and how he could *get* to know her, since she was gorgeous, after all, and obviously in the mood for something. "Well, I'm looking for a guy named Max. Do you know him? Have you seen him?"

The covers stopped. "You mean *Cynthia's* Max?" she asked.

"Yes," he said, more focused, "that's the one."

"I mean, I've never met him," she said, dreamily. "But she's told me a lot about him and I hope to someday."

Jack's blood began to boil. "Why? What's so great about this Max freak?"

"Well, for one thing," she said, "he has the reputation around town of being better in the sack than just about anyone." She paused for a second to release a high-pitched squeal. "But I don't have any direct experience, you know, with him, in, you know, that area."

"So," he said, steaming, "you haven't seen Max."

"Oh, Max?" she asked, like she was reconsidering the question. "Oh, yeah, I've seen Max. But he's a dog…an Irish Wolfhound. Wait; is *that* the Max you're looking for? Why didn't you say so?"

He stared at her like she was a total moron. "No, no… Hey, wait a minute. Weren't you at Steven Sternberg's place? Wasn't it your evil little dog that attacked me?"

"Evil little *dog*? Steven Sternberg? The big movie director? No, no, I would definitely remember that. I *heard* about it. That was something. Wow, I heard he bit you right in the… are you okay down there?"

"No, he only bit my leg. I'm totally fine."

"Are you sure? I've heard rumors that, you know, you're not

as, how should I put it, substantial down there as you used to be."

"What? No, untrue! Where did you hear these rumors?"

"Gee, I don't know. I think I read it somewhere or saw it on TV or something. *Extra!* Maybe? They had photos and everything. Did you have to have reconstructive surgery?"

"No! It was just my damn *leg!*" Jack was beginning to lose it.

"Just your damn *leg?* That's what you call it to overcompensate for your loss? Don't worry, your secret's safe with me. They can work miracles with grafting nowadays. But, no, I wasn't there. You might be thinking of my twin sister, Lolita. I'm Lila."

Lolita was breathing heavily now. She was on the verge of climax.

Jack was breathing heavily now. He was on the verge of a nervous breakdown.

"Listen. If you come across that Max guy will you let me know?"

"Are you talking about the dog now, because, like I said, I don't know Max, the man."

"Please stop talking!" snarled Jack. He looked at the TV again, shaking his head. "*Clooney.*" He picked up the remote and clicked off the TV, Clooney blipping into darkness. Jack quickly exited, sure that this "Lila" person was totally insane. And totally disgusted by her taste in men.

Max Ramsey immediately popped up from under the covers, twisted his neck until it cracked, and laughed. Then he climbed aboard Lolita and lunged dick-first for Lolita's little pink Vespa. She let out such a piercing squeal that Jack stopped and looked back, listening for a moment through the wall.

"Fucking Clooney," he snarled.

He tried the next door.

Locked. God damn it. He pounded like hell until the door opened.

There stood Paloma, partially dressed, with all the best parts showing.

"What *is* it, Jack?" she cried, ready to fight.

"Paloma? Oh, thank God, it's good to see you. Have you seen that Max Ramsey guy, Cynthia's brother? He's here on the boat somewhere...have you seen him?"

But before Paloma could answer, Seamus emerged from the bathroom. "Max Ramsey?" he asked. "Wait, you're Jack Stone? What the hell is Jack Stone doing here? You know Jack Stone?"

"The real question is, what are *you* doing here?" asked Jack, leaning in close to Seamus.

"Calm down, Jack," said Paloma, pecking him on the cheek. "This is Seamus, my *boyfriend*. Seamus...my mother was Jack's assistant for years..."

"That's true," said Jack. "But I'm also..."

Paloma interrupted again.

"We met in Mexico when he was working on a movie and I came along with my mom. I must have been, I don't know *sixteen?*"

"No," said Jack, "you were not sixteen!"

"You're right," she replied. "More like fourteen."

This shut Jack up.

"Jack's like an uncle to me. Or a grandpa. I guess tonight he's more like a *cranky* grandpa."

He was pretty sure Paloma had been twenty-one at the time, but he realized he was far from certain.

"Well," said Seamus, "it's a great pleasure to meet you, Mr. Stone. I have a screenplay you might be interested in."

"Well..." said Jack.

"He'd love to read it, wouldn't you, Jack," said Paloma.

"Well..." mumbled Jack.

"That's fantastic!" said Seamus. "I've got it in my duffle

bag. I'm confused about one thing, though."

Paloma and Jack froze for a beat, then Seamus continued: "*The Long Way Home*. What the hell happened there?"

Jack walked out without saying a word.

Seamus looked at Paloma without saying anything for a moment. Paloma laughed a little, then laughed a little more. But Seamus wasn't laughing.

"What is it?" she asked.

"Paloma. I have a question for you too." He opened his wallet, took out the little piece of paper, and held it up. "Tell me the truth, are all these Jacks——the ones with the hearts drawn so lovingly around them——are all these Jacks Jack *Stone*, by any chance?"

Paloma's mouth fell open in an expression of surprise and horror. But then she laughed a little again.

"I cannot tell a lie," she said. "Yes, all five of those Jacks with all five of those hearts are indeed Jack Stone."

"That's kinda what I thought," he said.

"But that is a very old piece of paper. Ancient."

"That's kinda what I thought too," he said.

"But...but..." she hesitated, not wanting to say the next part, but wanting to also. "I was still seeing him until very recently. I'd wanted to stop for a long time. But I didn't until just a few days ago."

"That's what I was afraid of. So why did you stop?"

"Well, because I met someone."

"But you know that's totally insane, right?" asked Seamus. "Completely bonkers. Unfathomable. It can't be possible that one of the biggest movie stars on the planet is out on the poop deck with dashed hopes while an Irish nobody with a pile of unpublished stories and a resume that fits on a single line of his cabbie license and less than a dollar to his name is in here with someone like you. You cannot be serious. Why would I believe you? Why?"

She looked at him. She loved his face. She loved his voice. She loved his touch. She loved how he'd held up the stupid piece of paper with those stupid hearts. She even loved that he'd asked why. Because she knew why.

She had been thinking about something Cynthia had said: *It's all about finding the right characters for the right story.*

"Seamus. It's because you are part of my story and I am part of yours. Jack Stone isn't. He's like one of those elements you force into a scenario in a ham-fisted way because for some terribly misguided, totally stupid reason, you think it deserves to be an integral part of things. And for a while anyway it feels like the story won't work without it. But then, after a few revisions, other more authentic things emerge, and that first thing seems phonier...less relevant."

Seamus interrupted: "But you still keep hanging onto it, because you can't quite picture the story without it. Then one day you realize you can't get where you want to go because you keep bumping into it, like it's an extra couch, a huge ugly couch covered in faux fur, right in the middle of your living room. It's a eyesore monstrosity that you obviously need to throw out, but it somehow seems heartless when you first think about that because it's been around for so long, you're accustomed to its utter ugliness, that's your very own disgusting couch, so how can you just heave it into a dumpster or something?"

Paloma: "And then comes mold and mildew and mice and possums and roaches and then one day a family of rats moves into the couch and you finally say *enough*. So into the dumpster it goes, and then all the way to the dump. Maybe even onto one of those garbage barges floating aimlessly at sea."

Seamus: "You don't need it. You won't miss it. You won't miss the fading stench of what used to be part of your story."

Paloma: "You've found something else. You've found

someone else whose story makes your story better."

Seamus moved closer: "So, just to be clear. International film star Jack Stone is an ugly couch, right?"

"Right."

"Covered with faux fur."

"Yes."

"And all manner of disease-spreading vermin."

"Exactly."

"On a garbage barge lost at sea."

"Precisely," she said.

He thought for a second. "A shitty couch lost at sea that we want to read my screenplay."

"Bingo," she said. "Do you think you can live with that?"

He shrugged his shoulders. "I'm pretty sure I can live with that."

He smiled as he reached down and slowly undid her blouse. She smiled too as she even more slowly unbuttoned his shirt. Then in silence, they took turns taking off pieces of each other's clothing in ultra-slow motion——pants/ skirt, underwear/underwear, stockings/socks——the delicate frictions of different fabrics tickling, bothering, activating their flesh, until they were naked, a little chilly, thoroughly goose-bumped, yearning for contact, all senses on high alert...

aching with desire.

He moved in close and hugged her, both shivering slightly, the sound and spray of the Pacific just outside the porthole in their cabin. He touched the exact spot around back where he knew the bluebird was, because even without seeing it he felt its happiness in his fingertips.

"In the interest of full disclosure, though," said Seamus, "as much as I am turned on by you, make that *aching* for you, and am quite possibly in love with you, I also intend to use you in each and every way I can to further my career here in Hollywoodland."

"Back at you on all that," said Paloma. "Except I'm going to use *and* abuse you."

"Well, yeah," he said, "that goes without saying."

"Okay," said Paloma, kissing Seamus and taking Mr. McFun in both her hands, "would you mind if we stop talking and let the games begin?"

"Like I said, McFun has a one-track mind." He lifted her up high, first kissing her stomach, then caressing her breasts with his face.

"That's what I...thought," she said with a slight quaver and sigh in her voice as she wrapped her legs around him and slid slowly downward... teasing, squeezing, and easing him in.

Chapter 35

One bottle down, another halfway there. Ava and Timothy had talked about everything, from art to music to life and love.

They were sitting together on the couch. Timothy kissed her tentatively, but sweetly. And Ava was in the mood for sweet. She was a little sleepy from the champagne. It was the good tiredness, though, the kind that just makes you relaxed and remarkably receptive to sensuality, like your nervous system is disarmed and available. He kissed her again, this time with more confidence, but still soft and tenderly... tasting, not hell-bent on consumption.

He moved to her neck and continued his gentle assault. In the two years since Jonathon died, several suitors had gone so far as to kiss Ava's lips, but none had made it to the neck. As tame as it seems, for her, after this long period of sensual deprivation, it was deeply erotic, almost the ultimate erogenous zone. Going further was almost unthinkable.

"Timothy," she said. "I know this is going to sound funny, but would you mind taking a bath with me?" She felt that, more than anything, she was looking for comfort, for some kind of sense of calm with a strong, kind, good man. She realized that she missed that so much. Out of the world of possibilities of human endeavor, she literally could not think of a single thing she'd like better than to fill up the tub and get in it with Timothy.

And that was what they did. They made the water too hot and easing into it over a period of minutes was bonding in and of itself. The tub was just the right size. Not too small to maneuver in and not so large that you float aimlessly from the edges toward the center, without anything to lean against. That was the worst.

He sat behind, straddling her, his arms around her, his erection pressed against her lower back. It felt so good there, just being there...sexual, sensual, and, again, comforting.

Skin so pink. Faces flushed. She was just about to say, "Timothy, would you mind washing me?" But before she opened her mouth, he was already washing her. First, her neck and shoulders. She realized that this kind of a massage was about a thousand times more effective than lying on a table being touched by a stranger. This was heaven. Soon she was wishing he'd move his hands around to her breasts, and suddenly they were there. He moved slowly, his hands slippery with soap. Her body was on fire...inside, outside, throughout. It was impossible to know where the hot water left off and body heat took over. It was the most supremely enjoyable sensation she'd had in a long, long time. She closed her eyes and just experienced it, living it, adoring it, feeling like it was all one could ever want.

And then suddenly it was not enough. Not nearly enough. Suddenly it felt like nothing more than prelude.

She slipped down deeper, the water to her chin, and turned her body over. Then she slid forward and kissed his chest, his stomach, then underwater, bringing her mouth to him, taking him in.

Timothy arched his back in pleasure. He hadn't expected this and it took his breath away.

"Ava," he said, kissing her forehead, "I think the bathtub portion of our festivities has outlived its usefulness."

She agreed. They stood up, both a bit dizzy for obvious reasons. He held her steady for a moment. He stepped out of the tub and as he lifted her up, she wrapped her legs around him. He moved slowly. Both were nearly overcome from the heat, but he eased her down slowly and began to make love to her, making her shudder, still dizzy, still hot, the perspiration mingling with the water, their fingers leaving white prints on their hot pink skin. She gasped as he lifted her and lowered her again and again, defining, then redefining the depths of her passion. Each time she cried out and each time it seemed like she had reached the outer limits of her inner pleasure, but each time the previous record was shattered, destroyed, forgotten...no longer relevant, no longer in the same league as what was occurring now and now and now. He leaned his shoulder against the door jam, pushing her back against the wall, and stood up on his toes, as if he would not be satisfied until he lifted her high into the air, floating like the sculpture in his loft, defying gravity, defying the finite dimensions of this room. She felt the sweet tremors building within and he felt her feeling it. She had loosened her grip on him when the wall had provided some stability and now she reached up and pushed her outstretched palms against the ceiling, pushing against it with her hands, while he strained upward, higher still. She began to lose herself, the muscles in her arms and legs quaking, rippling. She let out a soft moan that quickly transformed into a high-pitched sigh, so wild and unworldly that it scared him a little, but his whole body was electrified. He pivoted toward the bed and paused for a moment, almost shaking.

Teetering...he held her firmly, his hands supporting her lower back as her upper torso floated freely, arms moving slowly, fingers trembling...

Timothy eased her up one more time, his hands lifting her buttocks, a trickle of perspiration across his lips, off his chin, onto her belly, and down into the spot where they were thoroughly conjoined.

Then over Timothy went like a tall tree whose roots could no longer bear its weight. And he landed, the hard penetrating deep into the soft and warm, the arrow finding its smallest, sweetest target, male and female furiously fused, pounding frantically and riding spasmodically, as if their lives depended on it.

Ava cried out with a whole new level of desperation and Timothy realized she was literally crying...sobbing, in fact.

"Ava," he said, holding her still. "Ava, are you all right?"

"Leda and the Swan," she wept, tears flowing, body convulsing with a seismic blend of euphoria and grief. All of her senses seemed to be overflowing at once. Timothy wondered if this all had been a mistake. Maybe she wasn't ready. Maybe he was in over his head.

"What?" he asked "Leda and the Swan? Like the Greek myth? Zeus and Leda?"

"Yes, yes," she whimpered. "The painting...so beautiful..."

Timothy was quite sure he had never witnessed this kind of outpouring of emotion in his life. He already knew that his heart was inexplicably tied to this woman he had only known for hours.

"What is it, Ava?" he whispered in her ear. "How can I help you, what can I do?"

"Oh, god. Oh, god. I miss him, I miss him so..."

"I know, I'm sorry," he said, kissing her face, salty tears telling the tale of her sadness. "Should I stop? What do you want me to do? I'm sorry, I'm so sorry." Timothy wasn't completely sure, but he thought his own tears might have mixed with hers.

"No, Timothy! No! Don't stop! I already miss Jonathon. Please don't make me miss you too. Make love to me until I stop crying. Kiss away my heartache. Kiss away my tears."

And then he let everything loose...great waves of joy and sadness, all of it was released. It seemed otherworldly...bigger, better, beyond orgasm. It was like some kind of deep sharing of everything, the good, the bad, the most beautiful parts of their deepest selves.

When it was finally over, it wasn't over. They both lay twitching, quaking, and wondering what had happened, what had hit them. The afterglow was a memorable incident in and of itself...more like *aftermath*. They were the survivors of a catastrophic event that may well have changed them forever.

"God damn," said Ava, thinking about wiping away the stinging sweat that had trickled into one eye, but unable to lift her hand. She couldn't move.

Timothy tried to speak, but his dry lips had fused together, resisting, and then finally parting just enough for three hushed questions:

"Why me? Why you? Why now?"

This was deeply existential...a serious question from a serious man about a serious experience. But it struck Ava as funny. Sometimes the meaning and grandeur is beyond comprehension. And yet she knew at least one answer.

"Cynthia," she said with a smile, which turned into a laugh, "It's obviously Cynthia."

"Hey," he said. "'Kiss away my heartache, kiss away my tears.' Was that a reference to the Roxy Music song with the line '*Dance* away your heartache, *dance* away your tears?' Just wondering."

Ava stopped laughing. "My, my, I guess it was."

They both started laughing again.

Chapter 36

Max had been telling Lolita about the big deal he'd worked out in Dublin. "If this goes through," he said, "I'll never work again."

"Do you work *now?*" she asked. She was totally serious.

"What do you mean?" he asked, slightly hurt, but only for one nanosecond. Max was ridiculously resilient. "Okay, well, no, I don't work very much and I don't work very hard, but, come on, technically, I *do work*. Sometimes. Way too much in my opinion. Anyway, when this deal is signed, I'll take you around the world. You can bring the dogs. I'm talking about life-altering money. Fuck-you money. Fuck-the-world money. Seriously."

"Sounds nice," she said. She didn't care about being obscenely rich. She did appreciate how nice Max was being lately, though, and she was touched that he would invite the dogs along. He understood that she could never leave them.

But she was also starving.

"Max, I'm famished. Would you mind running over to the dining room and snagging me some of that lobster salad? I need to get my strength back if you want to screw the living daylights out of me again. Living daylights in, or living daylights out: your call." She pulled the peach, almost flesh-colored satin sheet over her nakedness, up around her neck, smiling coyly and leaning back onto pillows. The contour of her breasts and nipples underneath was more overtly sexual than actual nudity.

"Your daylights are going to be scattered from here to Catalina," he said. He would risk a thousand deaths for another round with Lolita tonight. He too had been reminded of *The Cat's Meow* and earlier, while doing what he did best, he'd started whispering to her clitoris, calling it Rosebud in honor of Davies and Hearst and one of his all-time heroes, Welles.

"Don't move, Rosebud," he said sweetly, bending down and kissing the gossamer sheet in the vicinity of Lolita's rosebud, pausing for a moment to breathe through the sheer fabric, warming the flesh below. "I'll be right back."

"You'd better be," said Lolita in a soft falsetto. Then, in her normal voice, "That was Rosebud talking."

Max pulled on his pants, went through the door, and gently closed it behind him. He took a few steps into the near darkness and came face to face with Jack Stone.

"Aha, so there you are," said Jack, his rage rising again. He moved threateningly toward Max, his arms crossed, his breathing heavy.

"Listen, man," said Max. "Why don't we just call this whole thing off, you know? Potato-potahto. What's the point of being angry anyway? I mean what good does it do anyone?"

Jack didn't say anything. He just moved closer, chin down, fists up, taking a boxer's stance. He had a good four inches of height on Max and who knew how many inches in reach.

"Because, you know," said Max, holding his hands up in sort of a what-the-hell non-threatening gesture, "when you come right down to it, it's really not a fair fight."

Still nothing from Jack except the slightest pre-fight slow-circular motion of the fists that denotes static energy about to be transformed into all out whoop-ass, face-pounding energy.

"Because," said Max, "it really wouldn't be very gentlemanly of me to pick on a mentally challenged person." Max could never resist a joke. Especially a dangerous one.

Jack shook his head and then swung hard, but Max simply stepped backward, narrowly avoiding the gigantic fist.

Unfortunately, he stepped on someone's toe.

It belonged to Seamus, who had come out on deck with Paloma for some brisk post-coital air.

"Excuse me, there, sir," he said politely. "Didn't see you there." But then Max turned around. "Wait," Seamus continued, his voice revving up an octave, "I know you."

"I don't think so," said Max, now moving away from two, count 'em, two angry revelers.

It was hard to tell which of them was more irate.

"This is the feckin' arshole who spilled his feckin' jiz all over the backseat of my feckin' cab!" Seamus said

"What?" asked Jack and Paloma and a few other partiers who happened to be nearby.

"Who the hell *are* you?" asked Max, peering into Seamus's face for a glimmer of recognition.

"Back in Dublin. You were getting your knob gobbled by a young Irish girl, kicking the back of my seat like a feckin' mule, slamming my feckin' head against the feckin' horn! All the while gabbin' on the feckin' phone to your feckin' girlfriend back in America!"

Lolita, just emerging from the cabin, raised an eyebrow and looked at Seamus, then Max. "Holy feck," she said. "I think that might have been me." She wasn't exactly surprised... just a little disappointed. *But what was she thinking? This was Max.*

Jack was trembling with anger and disgust. "IT WAS PROBABLY HIS SISTER!"

Everybody stopped, wondering what the hell he was talking about.

"God, Jack, I'm beginning to wonder," said Lolita, pointing to her head and his crotch, "are you mentally as well as, you know, physically impaired?"

"Shut up, Lila! It was just my *leg!*" he growled, causing everyone to wonder about him even more.

Jack lunged at Max, who turned to run, but Jack grabbed him in a bear hug from behind and lifted him off the ground.

"Hey! Come on! What the hell!" said Max, trying to wriggle free.

"Jesus, Jack, you asshole!" screamed Lolita.

"Lila, I said *shut up!*" snarled Jack, squeezing Max tighter and staggering across the deck. He hoisted him up, and balanced him on the side rail, clutching his collar, holding him in place...threatening to tip him over the side.

Seamus stopped in his tracks. Where was this going? "Jack, I think maybe it's time to calm down," he said.

"Yes, Jack," said Paloma. "Must you always be a dumb ass?"

"Face it, Jack," said Lolita. "Even a self-obsessed movie star has to consider the consequences of his actions once in a while."

Summer and Tatted Max tried to come to Max's aid, but Jack jabbed his index finger at them, keeping them back, barking, "Stay right there," and leaning Max slightly more seaward, the rushing wind and roaring ocean making everything seem even more prone to calamity.

But then suddenly, there on the deck, not twenty feet away, appeared three angry dogs. Where they came from was anybody's guess. They were glaring with alarming intensity at Jack, breathing and snorting like three prize bulls facing down an amateur matador. They hated him almost as much as they loved Lolita. And Max. They growled and drooled threateningly, making it clear that they did not approve of what Jack was about to do. The growling grew louder and louder. It almost seemed like they had some kind of weird three-part harmony going, like shape-note, sacred heart singing, vibrating in and slightly out of pitch, warbling into the night.

"Jesus, Mary, and Kujo," blurted Seamus. "It's those evil dogs again."

"They're not evil," laughed Lolita. "They're my babies."

But Jack was utterly petrified. He let go of Max and backed slowly away from the rail, holding up his hands like a cowboy with a gun in his back. When he reached a safer distance, he sprinted down the deck, hiding behind the mast.

Just then, a phone rang. Still perched upon the rail, Max, steadying himself with one hand, retrieved his phone from his pocket with the other. It was a Dublin number. "Hold on, everybody, hold on," he said. "I believe my Irish ship has just come in." He looked around at the yacht and the sea. "Ship. Kind of ironic. Hello?"

It was instantly obvious from the look on his face that it was not the call he was expecting. But this was Max. Even in the face of death, his charm was unstoppable.

"Emily! How nice to hear from you!"

Something clicked in Seamus's head. "Emily!" he blurted. "The girl from the cab!"

A woman in the back seemed to react to that information.

She stepped forward out of darkness.

Max saw that it was Molly Hannigan. She was dressed in a long, black raincoat, looking a bit zombie-like. Her eyes were vacant, shoulders hunched, one hand plunged deep into the pocket of her coat, causing the familiar protrusion in the fabric...the universal symbol for one thing only: gun. She had the pistol. She was coming for Max again.

"Hold on, Emily, we have a situation here," he said. "Molly, dear, please don't do anything you'll regret."

But Molly didn't say anything. She still had that same deadeye look on her face. She took another step closer. Max checked Molly's hand, twitching nervously inside her pocket.

Something bleeped in Max's ear. Call waiting. Another Dublin number.

Molly reacted again, taking another step toward Max, Night-of-the-Living-Dead-like...her hand and pocket twitching more noticeably now.

"Hold everything, Molly, everybody," said Max, "I've gotta take this other call. Molly, please hang on. Don't move. Don't do anything rash. I'm sorry about everything that happened. I'm sorry about all of it. And Emily? I'm sorry to you too. But please stop calling me. Okay, goodbye. Hello? Yes, Brian? Hi, yes, I'm good. And you? No, this is a very good time." He smiled slightly at the absurdity of that statement. "Oh, really? Oh, that's wonderful! Fantastic. That's very good news. Thank you. Congratulations to you too. Okay, yes, let's talk more later. There *is* actually quite a lot going on here at the moment. I'll call you back. Okay, thanks again. Goodbye."

Max smiled and looked at the people surrounding him in a semicircle on the deck...friends, enemies, ex-and-current lovers, totally entertained, baffled, and horrified strangers. "You will not believe my good fortune," he said. "I just got some very good news..."

But Molly stepped toward him again, faster this time, pulling her hand out of her pocket and thrusting it in his direction.

Max jumped over the side.

Lots of screams, a loud "AHHHH," a tiny splash, and Max Ramsey was in the drink.

Wilfredo, King, and Max the dog all dived in, Rin Tin Tin-style, after him.

Lolita let out a scream that made the other screams seem like whispers.

Molly Hannigan ran to the rail, dangling a set of keys at Max, below. "Your car keys!" she cried. "I'm just returning your car keys!"

She threw them over the side in his general direction.

"Don't worry," said Summer Starlight Friedman, "it's a rental."

And then Molly climbed the railing and leaped overboard.

Up on the quarterdeck, Cynthia and Captain Winslow, had been engrossed in a conversation about the burdens of leadership and the difficulties of long distance relationships. Turned out the captain had wed four times, but only his marriage to the sea had lasted. Going on thirty years. This was one depressing tête-à-tête. Finding out that you and a salty old sea captain have frighteningly similar romantic destinies is not exactly a happy discovery. Birds of a feather commiserating together.

"Man, woman, and dogs overboard!" they yelled.

Everyone rushed to the rail to see them all bobbing and flailing, then doggy paddling on the gently swelling sea.

Sailors scrambled across the deck, shined a searchlight down into the darkness, and threw a lifeline to the five water-treaders who were soon trailing behind the Que Sera Sarong like a troupe of water-show entertainers.

Cynthia descended the stairway to the main deck, shaking

her head. "I knew something like this was going to happen."

"The Dog's Meow," said Timothy, emerging from the cabin, hand in hand with Ava.

Cynthia smiled. "I thought you two might hit it off."

"You have no idea," said Timothy.

Ava moved in close to whisper in Cynthia's ear: "We took a bath. So comforting."

"Oh, Ava, that's so sweet."

But Ava wasn't finished.

"And then he kissed away my heartache, and kissed away my tears."

"Wow," said Cynthia. "Quite the testimonial." The heartache line sounded vaguely familiar, but she couldn't quite place it.

The crew hoisted up the dogs and Molly with a winch, but everyone thought it would be safer for Max the man to remain in the Pacific Ocean among the sharks, than to come back aboard.

"Hey, Ramsey!" shouted Seamus with a cheerful load of *feck you* in his voice, "Thanks for the hotel stay and the feckin' Starbucks!"

Max was mystified by this strange statement from the enigmatic, spirited Irishman, as was everyone on board.

Except for Paloma, who was getting an inkling of what had transpired. She liked his resourcefulness. An asset in Hollywood. She walked over to him and kissed him, mostly because she really, really liked him. But also to send a message to Jack, in case he was watching from wherever he was hiding, that their chapter was over for good. She had seen him more clearly than ever tonight and despite his fame and fortune and physical beauty, he was really not all that attractive. She'd been coming to this for a while, but always said to herself, *Come on, it's Jack Stone*. At the end of the day, though——literally *this day*——she could not imagine ever saying that to herself again.

Seamus was a much better bet. Maybe they *could* team up. Maybe Jack would read his script and get it to someone. Or maybe Seamus could direct the film version of *Going Down in the Valley*, or *Porn Free*, or whatever title they settled on.

Captain Winslow phoned his son, who immediately headed out to pick up Max. It took him a while to get there. Max was one salty prune-fish when Paul hauled him aboard.

"Ahoy," said the kid. "Just wondering, matey. Are you off your meds?"

As everyone watched them motor away, illuminated by the deck lights of the cigarette boat, they wondered why skipper and passenger were laughing so hard, and then, why Paul was screaming with joy. And they especially wondered why Max was in such a good mood, despite the fact that he was nearly killed and presently coughing up gallons of seawater and seaweed.

Except Cynthia and even Lolita. They got it. They were laughing too...at him *and* with him. At Max's good humor in the face of death and destruction. He was amazing like that.

Cynthia wished she'd had a chance to at least catch up with him a while. She loved hearing that bit about the cab in Dublin. She had been that girl in that cab and she was happy it wasn't her this time. And likewise, Max and her roles had often been reversed. No matter what anybody said, the guy had a certain purity of purpose about him.

Despite everything, Lolita wished he could have stayed a little longer for that second round. She had no illusions about Max whatsoever. For her, his upside was just as genuine as his downside. The dogs loved him. That was huge for her. And he really did seem like he was going through something. Some kind of change, maybe for the better. But sometimes change isn't easy even when you want it.

"Max! Call me!" she cried, waving at the shrinking boat until it vanished in the dark.

Cynthia put her arm around her. "There goes one funny sisterfucker," she said. Then she realized that Molly Hannigan was standing close to them, shivering, wrapped in blankets, like she wanted to talk.

"I believe I need professional help," she said.

Cynthia and Lolita both put their arms around her, showing her some much needed tenderness and sharing the names of much needed therapists.

The three of them spent the rest of the night talking about everything, absolutely everything.

Chapter 37

SUNDAY MORNING

Cynthia was beyond exhausted on the drive home that morning. She felt like she might actually fall asleep at the wheel, so she put the top down and let the wind whip like a refreshing tornado through her hair. She was still wondering how Lolita's dogs got on board the yacht. Three more wonders of the world apparently. And definitely talented and protective——even if they were almost always problematic. But in any case, essential to her best friend's well being, which made them essential to Cynthia's well being as well.

She tried calling her mother again and reached her in a hotel room in Venice.

"Bon giorno!" she answered, sounding incredibly happy.

"So, Mom, what's up with Dominic?"

"What do you mean what's up with him?"

"I mean, you know, the marriage, all those kids out of wedlock, you know...what's up with all that?"

"I feel like you're being critical of me, sweetie. Hold on."

"Mom?"

"Yes? Sweetie, hold on a second."

"What's going on over there?"

"Nothing, honey."

Cynthia could hear Dominic in the background.

"Is Dom there? Did he say something about getting going? I mean you're on vacation."

"No honey, it's okay, we're just hanging around the hotel today."

"So when are you coming home?"

"Not sure, honey. Dominic has a ton of air miles. We might just keep going for a while."

"Okay, Mom, I'm just going to come out and ask you. How do you see this working out?"

"What do you mean, honey?"

"I mean with Dominic."

"Easy. He adores me. He worships me."

"Yeah, but Mom, he has never been faithful to any woman

he's ever been with!"

There was a long pause.

"Mom? Are you there?"

"Yes, dear. Hold on a second."

Cynthia heard Dominic whispering something, then moaning something, and then howling bloody murder.

"Mom, is everything okay?"

"Oh, yes, honey. Everything is very okay. And to answer your question, apparently there are certain things I know how to do better than any of those other girls Dominic's been with. There, I said it. And we make each other laugh. Plus, I am never, ever letting him out of my sight."

It took Cynthia longer than it should have to figure out the nature of what was happening on the other end of the line because it was her mother.

"Okay, Mom, goodbye," she said, dropping the phone, which bounced on the passenger seat and onto the floor.

Boundaries, Mother, boundaries.

But then she laughed and felt happy for her. Maybe she *could* keep Dominic in line. Stranger things have happened. Not *much* stranger, though.

Cynthia noticed that she had a bunch of voicemails and listened to them. As usual, quite a few happy clients this weekend. Above all, Ava and Timothy seemed good to go and, who knows, they still might want her help in creating a new circle of friends *without* benefits.

Cynthia drove by the coffee bar on Franklin and thought about Seamus. He was a good kid and she hoped he'd hit it big in Hollywood. She thought he might have a better shot at acting than writing, but who knows? She would stop in tomorrow morning to say hi to Donald and Adriana. She hoped it would work out between Seamus and Paloma. They seemed like the right characters in the right story. She had no idea that she'd played a major role in bringing them together.

She turned up the hill and rounded the bend to her driveway. Someone was sitting on the steps.

It was Pete.

He had gotten sick and tired of all the miscommunication. He'd talked to the band and found a replacement for two weeks. He'd dropped his stuff off at his house and walked back down the hill to wait for her.

"How long have you been here?" she asked.

"About three hours," he said.

"Why didn't you call me?"

"I did, about fifty times. You didn't pick up...or bad

reception at sea. Whatever. I didn't feel like leaving another message that would probably come out wrong and make things even worse."

"Okay, I can see that," she said, kissing him and handing him her suitcase as they went inside.

"Two weeks, huh," she said. "You know, I don't think I can take this long distance thing anymore. It's impossible. It's frustrating, unfulfilling, maddening, and lonely. I want you here. With me. At least most of the time."

"I know. I agree. But unfortunately, all I have is two weeks right now. This tour just got extended for two more months. So we've got four more left in total. It's just the way it is."

"Yeah," she said. "But the way it is sucks. Do you want a drink or something?"

"I'll take the *something*," he said, touching her already glowing cheek——her telltale sign——with his fingers, brushing her hair from her face. "The whole time I was gone, when I closed my eyes, I saw you. Those lips. Those eyes. That brain. I know two weeks isn't much, but it's a whole lot more than we have ever had. Feels like a lifetime."

"Nice speech, handsome," she said, taking his hand, kissing it, and sliding it under her blouse and onto her breast. "It's a total crock, but it's a total crock I can relate to."

He smiled and unbuttoned her blouse, quickly dispensing with the bra and smothering every inch of her torso with warm, wet kisses before silently unzipping and letting her skirt drop to the floor. One hand still on one breast, the other moving along her ribs to the small of her waist, to the slope from hip to belly and downward, he kissed her softly, then deep and slow.

She reached into his trousers and reacquainted herself, instantly inspiring his kisses to become much more passionate, more serious...more meaningful.

There was something about the way he did what he did that was different. Something about his touch...something indefinable. Whatever it was, it was better...better than almost anything in the world.

They moved toward the couch, the rest of their clothes falling away, except for her maddeningly stubborn thong, which had become entangled between two of her toes. He removed it with his teeth.

But she stopped him when he started to lower her down.

"Wait, Pete, wait. I have a question."

"Good, because I have all the answers," he whispered.

"No, really. I'm serious. This might seem silly, but will you take a hot bath with me later?"

"I'll take a hot bath with you all day long," he said, kissing her neck, making her shiver slightly.

"Will you soap me up all over and rub against my hot, pink tingling skin with all of your body parts?"

"Every single one," he said. "No exceptions."

"Very good," she replied softly and sweetly, but also sort of like she was detailing an itinerary in a business meeting. "Okay. One: I'll call Paloma to tell her she's going to have to do a whole lot of filling in for me. I predict she will say, 'Yes, Boss. No problem, Boss.' And two: aside from an occasional bath and maybe a meal here and there, would you mind playing "hooky" with me nonstop for the next two weeks?"

"Let me think. Yes, this is an assignment I'd be pleased to take on and apply myself to with great dedication, Ms. Amas," he said, carrying her to the bed. "I promise to rise to the occasion whenever called upon."

She felt like he was levitating her. He was clearly a magician. She closed her eyes and floated gently downward as if drifting through a cloud painted by Marc Chagall. Or like they were those intertwined figures suspended from the ceiling of Timothy's loft...with the great sweep of Los Angeles and the Pacific below. She felt like a work of art. And for the upcoming admittedly too-short period of time, someone would be appreciating her as such. She craved deep comfort and earth-shattering pleasure, goddamn it.

Somehow Cynthia knew that she and Pete would find a way to navigate this relationship. Four months was only a heartbeat in a lifetime. Maybe, just maybe, she had finally found her own perfect match.

"Okay, Guitar Boy," she said, "just how much can you make me miss you when you go?"

The End